A CHARMING FATALITY

A Magical Cures Mystery

Book Seven

BY
TONYA KAPPES

D1706763

TONYA KAPPES
WEEKLY NEWSLETTER

Want a behind-the-scenes journey of me as a writer?
The ups and downs, new deals, book sales, giveaways and more? I share
it all!

As a special thank you for joining, you'll get an exclusive copy of my
cross-over short story, *A CHARMING BLEND.* Go to Tonyakappes.com
and click on subscribe in the upper right corner to join.

JUNE HEAL'S CHARMS

The list of June Heal's charms and what they mean:

- Turtle Charm = Be Sure and Steady On Your Journey
- Silver Owl = Wisdom, Mysticism, Secrets
- Purple Stone In Mesh = Clarity and Awareness
- Angel Wing = Guidance From Above and Protection
- Dove Sitting On a Gold Circle = Devotion and Hopefulness
- Third Eye Charm = Peer Past Illusions
- Small Potion Bottle = Harm To None

CHAPTER ONE

"A re you sure you have all of this under control?" Without making eye contact, I unscrewed the top off the Strychnos Nux-Vomica and held the bottle of the liquid substance over the boiling cauldron, silently counting one, two… ending in eight. I watched as the drops expanded into the mixture.

Immediately the substance began to bubble, turn murky and become a thin fluid turning rose in color.

Faith Mortimer stood next to me. Her onyx eyes focused on the cauldron. She brushed back her long blond hair behind her shoulder, her voice rose an octave, "Are you going to drink that for a stomachache?"

"I sure am." The boiling subsided as I stirred the potion with my ladle.

"I think I'd just run over to The Gathering Grove and let Gerald fix me up something a little more appetizing." There was a trace of laughter in her voice.

Only I wasn't amused.

"Listen." I set the ladle down next to the cauldron. I looked at Faith. My face grew still. "If you don't think you are going to be able to handle running the store while I'm working the couple of days a week at Head To Toe Works headquarters, I'll gladly find someone else to do it."

"Not at all." Faith stuck her head over top of the cauldron and took a nice long sniff of air. "Smells so good and looks delish!"

"You are so full of it." The cauldron shut off, telling me my home-made potion for the case of the nerves was ready.

It was my first day at Head To Toe Works, a national chain owned by Tiffany and Burt Rossen. They had been tourists in the magical village of Whispering Falls, Kentucky where Tiffany stumbled into my shop, A Charming Cure, needing a special cure to deal with her mother-in-law over Christmas.

Homeopathic cures were my specialty in our special little village. We might as well call a spade a spade. I am a witch—spiritualist was really how I liked to refer to myself—and I made potions. To the customer, I referred to my potions as homeopathic cures so it wouldn't scare them away. In fact, our whole village referred to each other as spiritualists and used our quaint shops to cover up our true witchy gifts.

"You are going to do awesome." Faith clapped her hands together. Her eyes sparkled. "You are the first to ever go outside of our village to expand your product."

"Yeah." I dipped the ladle down into the cauldron and took my first sip.

Faith was right. I was the first spiritualist who was actually going to sell products nationally and if not done the right way, I could expose our heritage and secret to the world. Only the world wasn't ready to know that real witches existed. They were content with reruns of *Bewitched* and *I Dream of Jeannie*.

It was such a big deal, the Village Council called the Order of Elders in to make sure the deal was legal and our heritage was kept a secret. To make things go smoother, I was going to give some of the profits back to Whispering Falls to help boost the economy. A lot was riding on my shoulders and the gurgle in my stomach let me know it.

Something had to calm my nerves and the Strychnos Nux-Vomica was just the herb I needed, along with the little extra dose of magic I had added to the cauldron. "That puts a lot of pressure on me."

Meow, meow. Mr. Prince Charming, my fairy-god cat, or some would say, my familiar, dotted his tail in the air toward the clock on the wall.

My eyes slid down the wall and focused on the framed photo hanging beneath it. The photo inside the frame was the only photo I had of my parents holding me as a little child. It was the only photo I had of all three of us. Just looking at it made my stomach settle a little more. I was determined to make them proud, even from the great beyond. For a split second, I thought I saw my dad's lip curl up into a big smile. I blinked, bringing my gaze back to the photo. Nope. No big smile. Just the smirk that was always there.

"Every bottle is filled and the shelves are stocked." I moved from behind the partition at the counter where I kept my cauldron hidden from the customers. "All the bottles have clear labels on them, so you should be good for the day."

I walked over to one of the many tables positioned around the shop floor, ran my hand over the red tablecloth and smoothed out a wrinkle.

"Make sure you. . ."

"Keep the tablecloths nice and make sure to fill up any empty spots on them with the bottles in the back room and those." Faith pointed to the wall where there were shelves filled with more bottles. "Don't forget about the shelves. Even though they aren't in your face like the tables, they get picked over and need to be filled too. And sometimes the bottles get moved around and you like the labels faced out."

"I'm glad to see you were listening." I tugged on the edges of the black and white polka dot dress I had decided to wear for my first day. "Are sure you don't need to get your work done first?" I asked, referring to her job as the editor of the *Whispering Falls Gazette* where she used her witchy gift of Clairaudience to communicate the news of the spirit world.

Clairaudience was the ability to hear things that are inaudible, making Faith the best candidate for the job. She could hear upcoming events in the whisper of a breeze or the rush behind a summer wind. She would then translate it and put it in the headlines of the Gazette.

"I have already recorded the paper for the day and it will go out around ten this morning." She pushed her shoulders back. Her face gleamed with pride.

"I'll let you know if I get it." I couldn't help but wonder if I would be able to hear the paper from the other side of Locust Grove, the town where I grew up, but also where the Head To Toe Works plant was located.

The Whispering Falls Gazette was not delivered in paper form. Only audible. Whoever subscribed to the Gazette got it delivered through sound, that way there was no trace of our little village secret to the rest of the world.

The knock at the door caused us both to look up. Bella Van Lou furiously waved from the other side of the window in the door. When our eyes caught, her lips parted into a big grin exposing the gap between her two front teeth. Her cheeks balled on each side, making her eyes squinty.

I rushed over and opened the door. The fresh smell of the summer wisteria vine that covered the front of my store wafted in, giving me a little extra calm to my stomach. The vine smelled especially potent today and I couldn't help but think it was Darla, my mother, looking down on me. She had planted those many years ago and I made sure I took special care of them. It was one of the last things living I had that she created. The other was a vial filled with wisteria vine oil that I had never been able to extract, so I kept special care of it as it was the special ingredient in my Gentle June's stress free lotion Head To Toe Works had contracted me to make for their national chain.

Other things, like some of the herbs she used when she owned A Dose of Darla, were still alive and well in the back of A Charming Cure. Those were my little secrets not to share with the world and I could duplicate those if I really needed to, unlike the wisteria vine oil.

Bella rushed in and I took one good deep inhale of the sweet fragrance before I shut the door behind her.

"I'm so glad I caught you!" Excitement filled her five-foot-two frame. A satisfied look came into her smoky eyes. "Here." She stuck her hand out and uncurled her fist.

Nestled in the palm of her hand was a tiny glass charm shaped like a potion bottle. Mr. Prince Charming darted in and out and between my legs in the pattern of a figure eight. His white hair was falling out all over my black heeled shoes with each turn around my ankles.

"You stinker," I said to him and took the charm out of Bella's palm. I held it in the air to get a good look at the liquid inside. "Look at the tiny liquid." I shook it and it filled with smoke. "What's in it and what does it mean?"

"It's my secret blend of Red Devil Smoking Hot incense, mugwort, myrrh, mandrake and witch hazel, a dash of bat blood and snake oil." She tapped the small bottle I held between my fingers.

"All in this little bottle?" I asked.

She nodded. "Collectively it means harm to none."

"How did you know what to put in there?" I questioned her ability to put together potions when her witchy gift was an astrologer.

Bella owned Bella's Baubles, the only jewelry store in Whispering Falls. It was interesting how she interacted with customers. They might come in for a fancy diamond, but it would enhance their life if they owned a different gem, so she'd talk them into the right gem to enhance their life.

"Him." She pointed her long finger down to Mr. Prince Charming.

He was sitting next to my feet, his tail swinging back and forth. I should've known. He showed up on my doorstep in Locust Grove on my tenth birthday. It was a dream come true. Darla and I didn't have a lot of money and the cake she had gotten me from the deli of the Piggy Wiggly had *HAPPY RETIREMENT* written in icing because it was on sale (the manager's special sticker was also a good indicator). Plus it took everything in Darla's soul to get me a sugary treat since she lived a holistic life. A treat was a rare occasion.

Mr. Prince Charming was snow white. He had a turtle charm with one green gem eye and one missing that dangled from his collar. Years later, I found out that Mr. Prince Charming was actually my fairy-god cat or familiar, who was sent by the Village Council of Whispering Falls to keep me protected because I was a descendant of Otto Heal, my spiritualist father and the sheriff of Whispering Falls who was killed in the line of duty.

Darla was not a spiritualist. But she had this shop, A Dose of Darla because she was married to my father. After he passed, she moved me to Locust Grove, the city next to Whispering Falls, to protect me. She moved the shop to the local flea market. She concocted her homeopathic cures in a greenhouse in our backyard where she grew her herbs.

It wasn't until long after my mom had died that the Village Council came looking for me, and told me about my past and how I belonged in the village of Whispering Falls where I could take full benefit from my heritage and create the real potions I was destined to create.

"Thanks, buddy." I bent down and picked up Mr. Prince Charming. I ran my hand down his fur before he jumped out of my arms. "You always know just the right charm."

"Yes he does." Bella confirmed and grabbed my wrist. She unclasped my charm bracelet and took it over to the counter, attaching the new charm to it.

My bracelet was filled with charms Mr. Prince Charming had given me. When we first moved to Whispering Falls, Mr. Prince Charming had dropped an owl charm in front of me. I had thought he had stolen it from Bella's shop. Only I found out that he and Bella had a little understanding that I didn't understand, but it was their witchy thing and not mine. I just went with it. As long as it protected me, I was good.

"You especially need protection since you are leaving the boundaries of our village and taking Gentle June's to a whole new level." She clipped it back on my wrist. She wrapped her hand around my forearm and shook it.

The bracelet jingled. Nothing fell off so we were good. But my stomach rumbled. Everyone was counting on me.

Another knock at the door caused us to turn our attention back to the door. Gerald Regulia and his wife, Petunia Shrubwood, stood on the other side, their baby nestled in Petunia's arms.

"Look at his hair!" I squealed, grabbing baby Orin and smothering his face with kisses.

"Tell me about that unruly mop." Petunia's eyes rolled. Her hair was in a peculiar array today. Most days she wore her hair up in a messy nest on the top of her head. Today it was half up and half down. Noticing me looking at it, she commented, "I just don't have the energy to fix it."

Petunia was the owner of Glorybee Pet Shop and her spiritual gift was talking to animals. Her husband, Gerald, owned The Gathering Grove Tea Shoppe. He was a tea leaf reader. They made a great couple and fantastic parents.

"I could give him a good buzz." Chandra Shango pushed her plump body into the shop, nearly knocking Petunia over. Her finger pointed to baby Orin. Her fingernails were polished blue with tiny gold stars painted on them. Chandra owned A Cleansing Spirit Spa, which was a cover for her spiritual gift of palm reading.

She was dolled up in a pink cloak and matching pink turban with a big purple gemstone in the center. Sprigs of her short raspberry colored hair stuck out of the bottom of the turban. She was rarely seen without some sort of head covering.

A black butterfly flew out of Petunia's hair and floated down to the ground after Chandra shoved her way through.

We stood in a circle around it in silence. We all knew what it meant without saying a word.

Death.

CHAPTER TWO

"**I**'m sure it means nothing," Petunia said in a voice that seemed a long way off. "We must be going." She took Orin from me.

"Yes." Gerald cleared his throat and handed me a cardboard cup. "We wanted to wish you well on your adventures today."

They rushed out, leaving the butterfly lying at my feet. Mr. Prince Charming batted it at, sending it close to the door.

Chandra didn't say a word; she just rushed out behind them. With one swipe of his paw, Mr. Prince Charming knocked the butterfly out the door before Chandra slammed it behind her.

I gulped.

"Stop it." Bella swatted the idea down that something bad was going to happen. "You go and have fun." She reached out and grabbed both of my hands, giving them a good squeeze. "You have all the protection you need right here on your wrist."

"Protection?" Oscar Park asked after he opened the door of the shop. "I'm all the protection she needs."

A vague sense of light passed between us when our eyes met. He was the love of my life and my future husband.

"If I can only get her to set a date to marry me." He peered at me intently. I saw the heart-rending tenderness in his gaze.

"I'll make it soon," I assured him. "Let me get this job started and see where it's going before I add more stuff on my plate. You aren't going anywhere are you?" I asked and brushed my bangs out of my eyes so I could take a nice long look at my handsome fiancé.

"You are stuck with me." His blue eyes sparkled against his olive complexion. His black hair had the perfect amount of gel in it. He had on a grey tee-shirt and jeans. He stood there, devilishly handsome. The rich outlines of his shoulders strained against the fabric of his shirt.

"And I have you to protect me." I batted my eyes, acting like a helpless lady, only they all knew better.

"You better get going." Faith pointed to the clock. "I'm fine," she assured me before I had the chance to ask.

"You are too." Bella's hands were clasped in front of her; she swayed back and forth.

"Okay." I was about to take the next step in my life. "You ready?"

Meowwl, Mr. Prince Charming growled. It was in my contract that he could come to Head To Toe Works with me. I couldn't go without him.

"And you?" I grabbed Madame Torres off the counter and grabbed my messenger bag.

"Are you kidding me?" Her face appeared in the center of the crystal ball. Her face pasty white, lips blood red, and her flaming red hair took up most of the ball. "It's way too early for me to do anything."

"Good. You can stay silent all day." I stuck her in the depths of my bag and placed it across my shoulders. I picked up the suitcase where I had made a travel kit for things I might need on the job.

I was going to be sharing one particular potion with Tiffany and Burt's company. A stress potion that was going to be turned into a lotion, so I had to have all the right ingredients.

Some of the contents included: an old scrying mirror, a black candle, black chalk, a box of matches, chunks of crystal and pyrite to enhance riches and psychic awareness, a vintage incense burner, a roll of charcoal tablets to burn incense, and of course, my secret blend of the stress potion Tiffany Rossen had fallen in love with during her snowed-in stay in Whispering Falls over Christmas. I also added photographic artwork and many magical vials, excluding the wisteria vine oil from Darla which I kept on the shelf behind the counter, and treasures for just in case I was in pinch situations. Though I didn't foresee or rather, my intuition didn't alert me of any danger.

"Are you sure you are going to be fine, because if you aren't." My hand gripped the handle of my little case. "Oscar will be right across the street."

"I'm fine." Faith assured me with a sweet smile. "And I'm going to be fine."

"Right across the street," I gestured over my shoulder at the Whispering Falls police department.

Oscar shared the sheriff's position with Colton Lance. Both wizards. On the days he didn't work in Whispering Falls, he was a deputy with the Locust Grove Police Department.

"Right across the street," Oscar said with laughter, mocking me.

"Oh, hush." I smacked him playfully before kissing his cheek. "I've never let someone actually work, work for me as in all day a few days a week."

"But I'm always your fill-in, so this is no different. Go." She rushed me out the door and onto the small porch of the shop. "Go put your magic all over the world. Make us proud."

"The world," I sighed knowing this was a big step for our little village. I was actually going to go out into the mortal world and deliberately perform magic in lotions for people to actually feel less stressed. This was a big step. No wonder my stomach hurt.

"Are you okay?" Oscar asked and put his arm around me. That wonderful smell of his circled around my nose and lifted my spirits.

"I'm great." I smiled to myself as I spoke. Excitement started to stir in my heart. "I'm really great."

"You are going to be great." The warmth of his smile echoed in his voice. He pulled me to him and embraced me. "I'm so proud of you. So let's set a wedding date so I can call you Mrs. Oscar Park."

"No pressure." I looked up at him and stared into his big blue eyes. His lips slowly descended onto mine.

My first day of work at Head To Toe Works headquarters was going to be fine. Just fine.

CHAPTER THREE

"Here we go." I opened the door to the Green Machine, the loving name I had given my '88 green Chevrolet El Camino. My cloak I had put on before I left the shop swung around me like a warm blanket.

Like always, Mr. Prince Charming jumped in and quickly found his spot on the dashboard on the passenger side. He curled up, letting the warmth of the early morning sunshine streaming down into the window warm his fur.

I looked to the left of the shop at Chandra watering her drowsy daisies and moonflowers in the window flower boxes of A Cleansing Spirit Spa. Then I looked into down at Glorybee where Petunia had Orin tucked in a pouch across her body as she feed Clyde, her pet macaw who sat perched up in the window on a display.

I looked right of the store. Arabella Paxton, owner of Magical Moments and the daughter of Gerald's first marriage, was touching each of the flower arrangements outside of her shop. She was a flower spiritualist. She was able to tell a lot about a person or even their future when her customer would pick a flower. She was truly magical and lovely. Plus the best dressed shop owner in Whispering Falls. She always wore the latest fashions. Her long hair flowed down the back of her black tee that she paired with a pink crinoline knee length skirt. Adorable.

Arabella was also the granddaughter of one of the Marys. Mary Lynn to be exact.

The Marys are the Order of Elders in the witch community. Past Presidents of villages around the world. They rarely show up but when they did, you knew something bad was going on or something needed to be put in order. That was why our Village Council had called them in to take a look at the contract between me and Head To Toe Works.

"It's your big day!" Arabella touched a funny looking plant I had never seen before. A mushroom sprouted at her touch.

"What is that?" My curiosity got the best of me.

"Shroomroot! Great for lots of things." She waved her fingers. "Have a great day!" She stepped inside her shop.

"Are you leaving?" Isadora Solstice yelled from across the street. She stood on the front porch of Mystic Lights. She was the spitting image of Meryl Streep. She never wore anything other than a crisp shirt with an a-line skirt with her black pointy laced-up boots. Today she was dressed head-to-toe in black.

"I am." I waved.

"You have Madame Torres with you?" She asked in her mothering way about my snarky crystal ball whom I fought with more than used as a familiar.

"I sure do." I patted my messenger bag before taking it off over my head and dropping on the seat of the Green Machine.

"I'll talk to you when you get back." She turned and headed into her shop that was a cover for her gift of reading crystal balls and seeing into the future.

In fact, Isadora, Izzy for short, was responsible for bringing Oscar and me to Whispering Falls. Both of Oscar's parents were part of the witch world and, long story short, Oscar grew up across the street from me in Locust Grove and Izzy knew exactly where to find us. She was the lucky one who informed us of our witch heritage causing me to pass out a few times over the course of the first week. Now I was old hat at it and embraced every single moment of my life.

By working with Tiffany Rossen at Head To Toe Works, I was going to be able to help the entire world with a stress free life by bringing a product using my purpose in life. At least I hoped I was going to.

I took one quick glance around Whispering Falls and put one foot in the car.

"Wait! Stop!" The exhausted voice of Eloise Sandlewood, Oscar's aunt, came from the distance near Glorybee. Her short red hair was a dot in the distance. Her arms flailed above her head. Smoke flowing behind her.

As she ran closer, I could hear the swish of her teal summer cloak shift as she hurried. Incense in her hand created more and more smoke.

I got back out of the car and she stood in front of me running the wand of smoke up and down my body.

"Be the light, light worker, a light within, inspiration, awakening, soul, white witch, witch, magick, heal the world, help others, oneness, book of shadows, meditation, love, peace, safety is your grace," she chanted a few times.

I closed my eyes and let the spell she was casting fill my nose and soak into my soul. Eloise was an incense spiritualist and I felt the closest to her since she was Darla's best friend and knew me before I knew me.

Every morning, before dawn, Eloise walks down the street with her incense cleansing Whispering Falls before the day even begins.

"I'm so glad I caught you before you left." Her soft voice made me open my eyes. She had the loveliest pale face with the most mesmerizing emerald green eyes.

"Thank you." My heart leapt. I was one lucky little witch who had a lot of people who loved her. "I'm so glad I saw you too."

Over her shoulder, Oscar stood in the window of the police station. He blew me a kiss.

"I don't have to turn around to know who you are staring at." She reached in her cloak and pulled out a smudge stick. "You must smudge the headquarters before you start work." Her brows drew together in an agonizing expression. "Do you understand, June?"

"Yes." I gratefully took the smudge. "I packed everything but a smudge stick."

Which was kind of strange since I was the one who performed all the smudge ceremonies in Whispering Falls.

"Now you have everything." She patted me. "My little protection cleanse will help you get through today and keep your feet planted," she said in an odd yet gentle tone that meant business.

I pulled her into my arms and gave her a warm embrace.

"Thank you," I whispered.

"And start thinking about this wedding to my nephew." She pulled away and held me at arms length. "I love you like a daughter, June Heal." She took a step back. "Why don't you come by for dinner tonight after work?"

"I think that sounds great." I knew I would have a lot to tell her and Oscar so killing two birds with one stone was perfect.

Eloise left as fast as she came. With her words of encouragement and her cleansing spell deep within me, I got into the Green Machine and started her up, not bothering Mr. Prince Charming a bit as he happily purred.

"I never thought we'd be back in Locust Grove making cures," I said to Mr. Prince Charming when we passed the old wooden sign heading out of Whispering Falls. It read *Come back to Whispering Falls, A Charming Village, soon!*

"We will be back tonight." I smiled, never happier to be part of both worlds that I adored so much.

CHAPTER FOUR

H ead To Toe Works headquarters was a big spread-out campus on the far west side of Whispering Falls. Not just anyone could drive up the compound drive and get in; there was a large security stand in the middle. One side was for the coming and the other side was for the going.

"Good morning." The man in the security guard uniform stepped out in front of the Green Machine with his arms extended out in front of him, palms out facing me. "Please put your car in park."

I did what he asked. His head looked side-to-side and down my vehicle. He waved to another man who was inside the block building situated in the middle of the road. The man emerged from the building with a long stick and big round mirror on the end. He stuck the mirror under my car and walked around the entire perimeter.

The other man motioned for me to get out of the car.

"You stay and be good," I said to Mr. Prince Charming who was now sitting ram-rod straight on the dash with his eyes following the man with the mirror. "It's a formality," I said as if I knew what was going on or even if Mr. Prince Charming truly understood me, but it didn't stop me from talking to him.

My eyes slid from him to the glow in my bag. Madame Torres was trying to tell me something. It was going to have to wait.

"Hi!" I bounced out of the El Camino. I stuck my hand out. "I'm June Heal and it's my first day."

His dark, hawkish face seemed never to have known a smile.

I smiled bigger. Any bigger and my cheeks would have popped right off my face.

He took his thick finger and scrolled down his clipboard.

Awkwardly, I cleared my throat. He was taking longer than he needed to. I popped up on my toes and glanced over the top of his clipboard. He drew it to him and looked at me. His eyes squinted in suspicion.

"Nothing under the car, boss." The man with the mirror went back into the building.

"Nope. Just me." I bounced on the balls of my feet with my hands clasped in front.

Mewwl.

"And him," I whispered and looked down at my fingers. I didn't want to look at Mr. Prince Charming. I could feel he was doing something he shouldn't be.

"Sorry. You aren't on here. Leave." There was no detection of thawing in his voice.

"But Tiffany and Burt are. . ." About that time a tall figure came toward me from the other side of the gate.

"June!" Tiffany called from the shadows of the tree line. She stepped out into the sun. She had on a pink jogging suit and a matching pink headband. There were ankle weights velcroed around each ankle, a small dumbbell in each hand. She pumped her arms up and down over her head with each step. The sunlight made her hair have glimpses of gold, adding a shimmer around her.

My intuition told me the stress potion I had made her was working and her appearance was showing that it was.

"Ronald! Ronald!" Tiffany waved the dumbbell in the air. "Let her in!"

"Ma'am, she's not on the list," Ronald held the clipboard in the air. "And Mr. Rossen said—"

"I don't care what Mr. Rossen said. I'm the boss here." She jutted the weight toward us as her pace picked up, inching closer and closer. "I said! You hear me! I said!"

"What is your name?" Roland's voice changed in tone to somewhat more of a pleasant nature of having to be nice.

"June Heal as in H-E-A-L, not heel like the foot." Every time someone asked for my name, it never failed; they would spell it as in the foot heel. This way it was up front and no miscommunication.

His brows pulled into an affronted frown.

"Shoowee," Tiffany stopped and handed Ronald the weights. He juggled them with the clipboard until he had everything in a football grasp. "Did you see those trees? Do you see how the sun is not coming through and the making all sorts of shadows?" She didn't wait for Ronald to respond. "I thought I told you that you had to cut those back. No shadows. Full sun."

"But Mr. Rossen," Ronald stammered.

"Mr. Rossen again?" She planted her hands on her thin hips. Raising fine, arched eyebrows, she protested, "This is my company and you take orders from me. I'm so sick and tired of him thinking he is in charge of my company. He thinks he is going to get this company, but it will only be over my dead body. You got that, Ronald?"

She didn't bother getting an answer from Ronald before she turned to me. She tucked her arm into mine, elbow-to-elbow, and leaned over. She whispered, "I'm so happy to have you here. We've had a bit of an issue since we talked, but you don't need to worry with that."

She jerked me toward the car and was talking a mile a minute without me getting a word in. Before I knew it, we were at the passenger side of the Green Machine. Her nose snarled when she noticed Mr. Prince Charming was sitting on the hood of the car with his tail dangling down over the passenger door window.

"June." She pulled me closer as if she knew Mr. Prince Charming could hear her. "Um. . ." she glanced over my shoulder, and then back at me. "We don't allow animals in the factory." She snugged me closer. "I mean imagine the bad publicity we would get if someone was rubbing on your fabulous stress lotion and a cat hair was in it."

I wasn't sure how she did it, but she snorted, eye rolled, and curled her nose at the same time.

"Oh," I pulled my arm from out of hers and stepped back. "I had no idea that was the case so I guess my time here is done."

Growl. Mr. Prince Charming stood on all fours and arched his back. His mouth slightly open and showing his premolars.

"Mr. Prince Charming!" I scolded him and he settled down. "Thank you so much for the opportunity. Only I do not go anywhere where my fair. . .Mr. Prince Charming is not welcome."

"Could you imagine the returns we'd get though?" She tried to get me to see her side; which was never going to work.

"Did you find any cat hair in your stress cream I made for you?" I asked and picked up Mr. Prince Charming off the hood, cradling him in my arms and scratching him behind his ears. "He was right there as I was making it."

"Well, no, but. . ." She bit the edges of her lip as though she were trying to come up with a good solution. "Oh, damn." She flung her hand at me but looked at Mr. Prince Charming. "Fine. But if I get one complaint."

"You won't," I assured her.

"Fine." She opened the passenger door and got in and rolled down the window. "Well?" She rested her elbow in the windowsill. "Are you going to come to work or not?"

"I guess I am." I rushed around the front of the Green Machine with Mr. Prince Charming in my arms and gave a quick smile to Ronald before I got in the driver's side and shut the door. I put the car in drive and with both hands on the wheel I pushed on the gas, driving through the now open security gate.

CHAPTER FIVE

"Everything is laid out exactly how the contract states." Tiffany tapped her brow with a hot pink handkerchief she pulled out of the jacket of her sweat suit. She wiped, talked and walked without missing a beat.

She opened the door to the company and gestured me to go ahead of her. I stepped into a world of pink and black patent leather. It took everything I had not to turn around and run. Not because my intuition told me, but this was not the type of girl I was. Not a girly girl surrounded by pink.

Rowl. Mr. Prince Charming stood between the getaway door and me as if he knew I was seriously considering running back to Whispering Falls with my tail tucked.

"What's wrong with him?" Tiffany's nose curled. It wasn't a happy curl. "I can't have him acting like that and scaring the employees."

Before I could protest, a squeal came from behind the sleek black leather counter with brass studs haphazardly placed all over the front of it.

"A cat!" The dark-skinned woman rushed over and grabbed Mr. Prince Charming before he could run for cover. "Little bitty itty baby." She smothered him in kisses.

She stood about my height, five foot eight, and wore her hair in a loose afro. She had on a black shirt, black slacks, and black non-slip soled shoes. The hot pink logo matched the Head To Toe Works logo perfectly.

"Put that down." Tiffany protested. "You will get hair all over you and bring it into the facility." Tiffany shook her head and her finger at me. "I told you this was not a good idea."

Tiffany walked over to the counter and grabbed a Head To Toe Works black shopping bag. I followed her over there and took Mr. Prince Charming from the woman.

"It will be fine." I ran my hand over him to make sure he was okay. "I'm June and this is my cat, Mr. Prince Charming."

"Nice to meet you." With Mr. Prince Charming nestled in my arms, she gave him another good scratch behind the ear, sending him into a purring fit. She looked down at her shirt and held her arms out to her side. "See, no hair."

"He doesn't really shed." I had never really thought about it, but he didn't. After all of these years, you think I'd noticed.

"Here." Tiffany held the bag out to me. "When you work your two days a week, you will need to wear the uniform like everyone else."

"Really?" I had never worn a uniform for a job and wasn't sure how this was going to work out. How did she know my size? I took the black pants out and held them up while the woman and Tiffany whispered between them.

"It's not right." The woman's voice was hard. "The bottles aren't nearly as cute and the plastic ones do not hold all the product."

"It's fine." Tiffany looked over at me with a sweet smile. "Aren't those adorable?"

"Adorable," I groaned pulling the stretchy waistband. I could already feel the painful indentions the ribbed band was going to make around my stomach. "Is there something wrong with my product?"

When the woman said something about the bottles, my internal intuition gift went off like an alarm. Something around here was off.

"Wassup?" Another worker walked into the building with the same exact outfit on, saving Tiffany from my question. "Dude, a cat." He reached his arm out.

It was hard enough not to stare at his nose ring and I couldn't help but notice the five-point star tattoo.

My eyes bolted open and I gulped. It was true there were many witches in the world. The Good-Siders and the Dark-Siders were the two classifications. We were a very segregated world until I had mistakenly been appointed to be Whispering Falls Village President, which I gladly gave up to Petunia.

Anyway, you could never be too careful and I wasn't sure if he was part of the spiritual world or not, but anyone who sports a symbol from my world always made me cautious.

Mr. Prince Charming stood on two legs, batted my wrist and darted around my leg when the tattoo guy tried to pat him.

"What's wrong with that cat?" he asked.

"He's a little shy at first." I didn't want Mr. Prince Charming to seem rude though I knew he was telling me something was off by batting my wrist. "I'm June Heal. I think we are going to be working together."

"Oh no." Tiffany extended her arms over her head and in one fluid motion swung them down and around in a stretch. "Josh works on the line." She tapped her watch.

"The line?" I asked. The man and woman both turned and walked away silently. "It was nice meeting you!" I called.

"Your contract states that we are only a co-packer for your line of stress free lotions. You have some attorney." She nodded. "The other contract was the one where you raked us over the coals for the percentage you will get in order to be featured in Head To Toe Works."

"Oh." I bit my lip. I had no idea what the Village Council had come up with in terms of the agreement. All I knew was that they had to contact the Marys, the Order of Elders, to get permission. And their decision was my decision. I had agreed to split half of the earnings to go back into Whispering Falls so we didn't have to go through another recession like the one we had gone through around Christmas.

"Follow me." Tiffany instructed, curling her finger behind her shoulder and walking while still talking. She opened a door and we walked through.

It was a long hallway with windows on both sides looking down into the factory part of the headquarters.

"The factory portion is built underground due to the nature of the creams. They have to have proper temperature and having it built this way provides a more constant temperature without using as much energy. It is greener and we are able to use the money saved to use the best nutrients and vitamins in the product." We stopped and both looked down on the assembly lines. "This is one reason why our customers love us so much."

"I see mine!" I was barely able to control my gasp of surprise when I saw the label being put on the bottles.

When I first agreed to the deal, I wasn't sure how much I would enjoy seeing my product out there. A lot of people had my product even before I started to produce it. Darla sold plenty of this same homeopathic cure to the customers at the Locust Grove Flea Market. In fact, this one particular cure was the reason they would come back to the market. The only difference was I put a special potion in mine and Darla couldn't.

The potion I used was a basic one with a spell that conformed to the customer. Unlike a customer coming into A Charming Cure where I could intuitively tell what the nature of their stress was and tailor a potion to their specific needs, this adventure had to be as basic as I could and yet enough to work so I could do my part for my beloved village.

"But. . ." I stammered when I noticed the extra special bottles, extra special as in where I had put the magic touch, were not what was being bottled, but rather still in the cardboard boxes I had sent from A Charming Cure. "Those are not my bottles."

"That is something I wanted to discuss with you." Tiffany's lips thinned. She looked at me with an intense but secret expression.

I flung the door open next to us and bolted down the stairs with Mr. Prince Charming next to me.

"No! No!" Tiffany hollered after me. She was so slow, I was already down the steps and in front of the machine.

"Stop this machine," I begged and ran around to the other side when I saw the dark skinned woman from the lobby. "Please stop this machine and use these," I begged and rushed over to the cardboard boxes and took out one of the special potion bottles.

I had taken the time to create these special bottles and hold them, giving each of them a special spell with my touch. Once the spell and the stress free potion, or lotion as they believed, mixed, the magical components of the product worked.

I held one out to the woman and shoved it in her hands. Her mouth was gaped open and an inexplicable look of withdrawal came over her face. She sat it down next to her and continued to place the cheap plastic caps on the cheap plastic bottles, sending them down the line to be packaged.

The tattoo guy kept placing the plastic bottles in the machine, letting them fill up with the stress free lotion I had sent. He shrugged.

"June, honey." Tiffany spoke calmly, with no lightening in her eyes, no smile of tenderness or even understanding to make me feel better. "If we were to carry those bottles, not only would we have to get special equipment, which is costly, but we'd have to up the price in the stores. It's all business."

"I don't care. I will purchase the new equipment." Though I wasn't sure how much it was or how I was going to do it. I just knew this was not right. "The magic won't work."

"Magic?" the guy asked.

"You know." I waved my hand in the air and rolled my eyes. "The reason my products sell so well is all about the packaging."

I thought I did a nice job of covering it up.

"Ouch!" I drew my hand back and rubbed my wrist. The liquid substance in the small potion charm was bubbling and hot against my wrist.

Mewl, mewl. Mr. Prince Charming stood on top of the belt on the assembly line.

"Damn cat!" Tiffany growled, slamming the palm of her hand up against the big red button to stop the product line, saving Mr. Prince Charming from going through and getting slimed with lotion. She drew her finger and screamed, "Get that cat out of here!"

"Why did you stop the line?" It was the first time I had seen Burt Rossen since he had come into my shop telling me how happy I had made Tiffany with my stress free products over Christmas time and her love-hate relationship with his mother over deviled eggs. "This will cost us money and it will come out of your paycheck!" He pointed directly at the woman and man.

"We didn't do it." The woman's eyes drew down. "Not that you care," she whispered behind his back when he walked past her.

"Mr. Rossen, I'm not sure if you remember me." I stuck my hand out. By this time Mr. Prince Charming was back at my ankles and the potion in the charm had stopped boiling. "I'm June Heal from the homeopathic cure shop in Whispering Falls."

"I know who you are, but you are in my territory now." He rubbed his bald head and looked around, not giving me the time of day.

"Please look at me when I'm talking. I'm not just a worker." I sucked in a deep breath. My name and product was on the line, it was time I took charge.

His eyes slid to mine. His features twisted into a maddening leer.

"You have my attention, Ms. Heal," he spat.

"I have spent several years perfecting my lotions and as your wife can attest, they work." Somehow I had to get him to get rid of the bottles he had already processed. "I didn't agree to put my name and lotion in such cheap bottles."

"If the product is as good as you and my wife claim, the packaging won't matter." His brows lifted.

"That is false. Statistics show that consumers will be more likely to pick up a nicely packaged product over . . ." Tattoo spoke up.

"Are you Head To Toe Works' marketing director now, Josh?" Mr. Rossen asked with a strong stamp of arrogance.

Josh's face reddened.

"I didn't think so." Mr. Rossen turned back to me. "Plus we have already co-packed over 200 boxes. We will not lose product. Do you understand?"

"Yes, sir, but this is not what I agreed to." I had to get back to Whispering Falls and talk to Izzy about the agreement the Marys had come up with. There was no way they would agree to different bottling, not if they knew what was on the line.

"Then we would have to get a larger belt for those types of fancy bottles." He shook his head.

"Not really." The woman with the caps spoke up. "We have that barbecue sauce that went south. Those were big bottles on the line over there." She pointed to the corner off in the distance.

"And are you in charge of bottling?" His face was hard, crude, and merciless.

"Burt, dear." Tiffany lightly touched Burt's arm. He stepped aside coming up to her shoulder. They were an odd pair. She whispered something in his ear. His chest heaved up and down with a big sigh and he looked directly at me.

"After these go through, we will switch machines. But that won't be until tomorrow. Got it?" He pointed at me. "These couple hundred boxes will be shipped out tomorrow as planned."

"That's my poky." Tiffany ran her fingernails up his chest and pinched his chin. It must've been their thing because I had seen her do this to him the last time I saw them at Christmas.

"You two," he gestured between the two employees, "you each now have a demerit."

"But," Josh protested. Tiffany shushed him quickly.

We stood there watching Burt leave.

"Get a leash on him," Josh (the tattoo guy) said to Tiffany before she glared at him.

Tiffany pushed the button to start the line again. In agony, I watched the few remaining fake bottles go through the line one-by-one getting filled up with perfectly good stress free magical lotion that was not going to be worth the two cents it was packaged in.

Slowly an idea germinated inside of me.

Burt said he wasn't going to ship them out until the next day which meant they would be stored in the warehouse until the trucks would be there to pick them up to deliver them to the stores. There would be a window of time I could come back and put a special hand on each of the bottles that were already packaged, giving them the special touch needed.

"Thank you," I said to Tiffany as we made our way back up the stairs to the offices. "I really do believe you will see a difference in sales with the real bottles I sent."

"I know. I should have consulted you first, but Burt has a way of making me believe in his ideas." She stopped and put her hand on my arm to stop me. "He has always been right. His ideas have always been spot on."

"But not this time." I tried to be as nice as I could, but anger boiled in me. "I know my product and I think you believe that as well." My intuition told me Burt was only in it for the money, which was a business and I got that, but that was not why I had decided to go national with this product. "Tiffany, I want to help people like I helped you. The cost was laid out in the contract. You knew how much your company was going to make using the bottles I had sent."

"Yes, but Burt knew we would have to get the special equipment that would fit your bottles on the assembly line." She bit her lip. "I never thought of using the old barbeque equipment. I really should have and I'm sorry it created a ruckus."

"It's fine." I most certainly didn't think it was fine. Now I had to come back and put a spell on those plastic bottles the lotion was already packaged in. This was a mess and certainly not how I had dreamed my first day would've gone.

"It's just that," Tiffany began to make excuses for what had happened, but I wasn't buying it. "Burt sort of oversteps his boundaries. He worked on the line after we met and I was just smitten with him. He had such a good business sense that I didn't have. All I knew was that I was a woman and I had to get good products out there for all women."

We took a few more steps before she stopped at a door with my name engraved on a door plaque. She opened it and gestured for me to step inside.

"He really does mean well. After all, he does put up with my little tantrums." Her words went in one ear and out the other.

When I stepped inside the room, I couldn't believe my eyes. The office was amazing. The grey palette and fluffy furniture was better than the furniture in my cottage. There was a large grey area rug with a diamond pattern in the middle of the room. A grey sofa was place on the edge of the rug facing the desk and behind the desk was the most amazing view of Locust Grove.

There was a kitchenette with a coffee maker and a pile of June's Gems on a covered pastry dish. A picture of Gentle June's Stress Relief was framed and hung on the wall in the exact bottle I had sent them.

"Gorgeous!" I ran over to the picture and gazed at it. It was the first time I had seen a promo.

"It will be in all the store windows and we did a big ad campaign in all the top national magazines," Tiffany's voice escalated.

"And this is why it is important to use my bottles." I continued to stare at it.

"But not at those costs with all the ads we are running." Burt trailed in the office behind us. "Listen, I know we kind of got off on the wrong foot, but I know business. Ask my wife."

"Oh, she assured me." I doubled over and put my hand on the edge of my desk to brace myself.

"Are you okay?" Tiffany asked.

I opened my eyes and looked down at the ground to see if I could get a reading on my gut feeling. Madame Torres glowed from the small opening in my bag. The potion bottle charm raged with boiling liquid. Something was wrong.

"I'm fine." I shook my head and stood back up. It was all wrong. But what? "I'm not worried now that we have the bottle situation straightened out."

"It's straight, but I'm telling you," Burt's voice escalated, he pointed his finger at me.

"Stop it," Tiffany growled and shoved his finger down toward the ground. "It will be fine."

He reached out and swung her face to him. "It better," he spat through gritted teeth and dropped his hand from her face.

"Hey!" Anger boiled deep in me. I sucked in a deep breath and envisioned my fist punching him as hard as I could in the gut. I had only been able to draw from this gift that was deep rooted in me once before. When I was a student at Hidden Hall, I was in a compromising situation and made a picture fly off the wall to knock someone out. Surely I could do it again.

"Ugh!" Burt doubled over. His face rose to mine. His eyes blazed down into my soul. I wasn't about to let him get the best of me. Even though I wanted to desperately look away, I knew I had to be the strong one here.

He stalked out of the office and slammed the door behind him.

"I'm sorry you had to witness that." Tiffany turned to me. The red marks on her cheeks told me how hard he had pinched her face when he grabbed it. "He really wants us to have the best life possible and truth be told, we are hanging on by a thread. There have been so many companies established, doing what we are doing and going overseas to co-pack or even make the product. I promised him that your product was gold and going to put us back into profits." Tears welled in her eyes. "You are our last hope. We have sunk every dollar into Gentle June's."

"Tiffany," a wave of apprehension swept through me. I wondered if I should keep my mouth shut, but I just couldn't. "You really don't have to put up with that type of abuse."

"Burt," she brushed it off, *pfft*, she waved her hand. "We can get a little loud, but I know he loves me."

"Are you sure because that didn't look like love to me." I sure didn't want to stick my nose where it didn't belong but I felt it was my duty to at least bring it to her attention that it wasn't normal for anyone to put their hands on anyone else. Especially the way Burt had done, leaving marks.

"Listen, we have invested a lot of money in your product. I believe in it and it's now time for the rest of the nation to believe in it. Burt is a little on edge because it's the most money we have spent on a campaign." Fear, stark and vivid, set in her eyes. "Ever."

She quietly turned and walked out.

One thing was for sure; I didn't have a good feeling about Burt Rossen. There was something about him that was off and it wasn't the fact he had just grabbed his wife who had obviously taken good care of him, but something I wasn't able to put my finger on. And I knew to keep a watchful eye on him.

I took Madame Torres out of my bag and sat her down on the desk.

"That was something." Her face appeared in the full globe. Her lips blood red, purple turban on top of her head, and green eye shadow across her eyelids. Her head swung around the ball. "I don't have a good feeling about this place."

I put my kit on top of the desk and opened it. My body felt weak. Almost helpless, but I knew there was a limited amount of time to get this place cleansed.

"Me either." My chest heaved with breathlessness. It took all my energy to pull the smudge stick out of the kit and I quickly put it back when the door opened.

Mr. Prince Charming darted in, Josh closely following.

"You settling in?" Josh walked in and looked around the room. "Nice digs."

"I thought so." My lips thinned as I watched his eyes zero in on the kit. I closed it and slipped it underneath the desk.

"Nice snow globe." He picked up Madame Torres and shook it.

"Please don't touch my stuff." I grabbed her out of his hands and held her close to my body. "Is there something I can help you with?"

"Nope. Just showing your cat where you were." His voice held suspicion. "I guess you got a good idea of how things work around here."

"I'm not sure what you are talking about." I channeled my energy into my gut, but my only problem was that I was exhausted from socking Burt in the gut with my mind. I eased down into the desk chair. My energy was zapped. There had to be some sort of quick recovery from the magic I had just done and I was going to have to figure out what that was.

"Ma'am." A security guard stood at the door. Josh and I both looked up. "Mr. Rossen asked me to escort you out of the building since your new start date is tomorrow."

Gladly. I grabbed my kit and stuck Madame Torres back in my bag.

"Let's go," I told Mr. Prince Charming.

CHAPTER SIX

"Well, that was a quick day of work." Faith was ringing up a couple of customers at A Charming Cure.

As soon as Burt told me on my way out the door that there was no reason for me to start today since the new packaging was going to start in the morning and the meetings we had on the schedule were postponed until then, I decided to come back to Whispering Falls. I could check on the shop, think about the wedding plans. . . think, and be at Eloise's on time for dinner.

"They packaged the wrong bottles." I shook my head and peeled my cloak from around my shoulders and put it on the coat rack next to the door. "I see some of the inventory has moved."

The shelves on the wall were refilled as I had asked her to, but the labels weren't facing forward the way I liked. On my way back to the register I went down the shelves and turned the bottles facing forward and arranged a few of the ones sitting on the table displays.

"Hi there." I greeted a woman standing in front of the sleeping aid display. A top seller for the shop. Her soft blond hair was pulled back at the nape of her neck in a loose bun. I didn't have to tap into my intuition to know she wasn't sleeping, the black circles under her pale, thin skin told me. But there was more to it and that was what my intuition told me. "Are you having trouble sleeping?" I asked.

Asking was the only way I was going to be able to get to the root of what she really needed. Over her shoulder I could see Faith was handling the register just fine and Mr. Prince Charming was by her side making sure. This was really a good thing. I was able to focus on the customer while Faith focused on checking the others out.

"I guess." Desperation set deep in her dull eyes. "I used to sleep so well, but since the baby." Her voice trailed off.

"Congratulations." I smiled thinking of Petunia, Gerald, and new baby Orin. "I'm sure the baby is worth all the sleepless nights."

"Oh, it's not the baby that wakes me up. I wish it were. The baby sleeps all night." Her mouth twisted and her eyes darted back and forth like she was keeping something from me.

"I'd love to help you but you are going to have to tell me what is keeping you up." I knew in my gut there was something else, but nothing was coming to me.

The smell of sweet roses streamed out of her mouth as she talked about her routine and going to bed not too early, but not too late as if I was going to tell her to change her routine.

"Do you love roses?" I asked.

Usually when I smell something coming from a client, it's because they love that something and I can alter their specific potion with that flavor, but the rose smell was so strong, I felt it was coming from somewhere deeper.

"Why would you ask that?" She blurted, scarcely aware of how loud her voice was.

"I thought I smelled roses. Maybe a perfume?" I smiled trying to get her to trust me.

"No. I hate roses, but my grandmother loved them. Her hand lotion was even rose scented." Her eyes held a little sparkle as she told me about her grandmother. "I loved my grandmother."

"Loved?" I asked.

"Yes. She passed before I had Rose," the intensity in her voice lowered.

"Rose." I sucked in a deep breath knowing her grandmother was present from the great beyond and knowing I couldn't help her. Dealing with spirits from the ever after was not my job. "Do you wake up every night at the same time?" I asked making sure I was on the right path with my hunches.

"Three thirty-three every morning. Like clockwork." She fiddled with her fingers. "I smell her. I smell roses."

"Rose, your daughter, is named after your grandmother's love of roses?" I wanted her to figure out where I was going with this.

"Yes. And every since Rose was born, I wake up to smelling roses at three thirty-three when baby Rose has slept through the night since day one. She's like an anomaly." Her cheeks had gotten a little more pink in them as she talked about Rose.

"What you need is a good massage with some homeopathic oils. And I have just the cure." I glanced over her shoulder and caught Faith's eyes. "I'm going to take her to see Chandra. I'll be back in a minute."

"I'm fine." Faith called, running her hand down Mr. Prince Charming's back. "We've got it covered."

"If you'll come with me, I know exactly what will let you get to sleep and keep you there until baby Rose wakes you." I motioned for her to follow me as we left the shop and went next door to A Cleansing Spirit Spa.

As soon as the doors of the spa opened, the smell of fresh linens and oils spread over us like a wave of water. It was known in the mortal world that spas used machines to pump in the homeopathic smells, but in the magical village of Whispering Falls, every sense, including your sense of smell was exactly what was dear to you deep in your soul.

"It smells like a bed of roses in here." The young mother took another deep breath, this time a smile covered her lips.

"Howdy do!" Chandra opened one of the spa doors from down the hall and greeted us. She adjusted her pink turban as her eyes zeroed in on the young mother. "Oh, a new mom."

"How did you know?" The woman pointed to Chandra. "How did she know?"

"We can see all, my dear." Chandra put her arms around her. The woman tensed, but that didn't stop Chandra. "Oh, we must get these knots out of your shoulders and get you sleeping." Chandra walked down the hall with the woman still curled in her arms. She glanced over her shoulder at me. "Thank you, June." She winked.

Chandra would do exactly what the woman needed. She would read her fortune and massage oils into her body. Obviously her grandmother had something she needed resolved from the afterlife and that was why she was continuing to wake her up in the morning. I also believed baby Rose never woke her mother because grandmother was probably soothing the baby. Unfortunately, I was sure I would see the young mother again because once Chandra revealed to her what the grandmother wanted, the grandmother would be at peace and baby Rose was going to have to be soothed by someone. The young mother.

The day was turning out to be lovely. The temperatures never got too hot in Whispering Falls since we were settled in the foothold of the mountains in our tiny village.

"I'm fine if you want to go on and go visit early with Eloise." Faith encouraged me to go.

"How did you know about Eloise?" I asked.

"She put an article in the paper about your wedding shower." Faith's brows narrowed. "Didn't you know about that? You didn't hear the paper?"

"I guess I didn't." Now that I thought about it, I didn't hear the Whispering Falls Gazette delivered to me. Not even in a whisper. "Strange."

"Strange," Faith's voice trailed off. "And everything was okay at the factory?" She questioned with a lingering anticipation of my answer.

"Not fine. Not even okay." Now I was getting a little irritated. I was hoping to go to Eloise's and throw her and Oscar a bone about the wedding. I really just needed time to get the new job under my belt before I made any wedding plans. I wasn't good under pressure, witch or not. "But you don't mind if I leave?"

"No, as long as you are paying me." Faith grinned.

"Of course I am." I grabbed Mr. Prince Charming off the counter and headed out.

I drove the Green Machine back up to our little cottage on the hill overlooking Whispering Falls with Mr. Prince Charming up on the dash. I loved my little cottage. It had the most spectacular view of the village. Plus it was near The Gathering Rock where we had all of our village meetings and the woods were right behind me, giving me easy access to Eloise and my Aunt Helena.

I didn't see Aunt Helena much since she was the dean of Hidden Hall, A Spiritualist University, which was clear on the other side of the woods through a secret portal.

She would definitely want to be included in my wedding plans since she was my only living relative.

Meow, meow. Mr. Prince Charming batted the air between us as if he knew exactly what I was thinking.

"You're right. No time like the present." It was all I had to say. He jumped off the dash, over me and out the door, darting around the cottage.

He and I both loved going to see Aunt Helena and getting some time in the woods.

I didn't waste any time. I grabbed my bag and threw it over my head, hanging it across my body and took off in the direction of the secret portal.

The sunlight darted through the tall trees in the woods and the scurry of animals' footprints could be heard as we made our way through, breaking fallen branches under our feet. Every once in a while, Mr. Prince Charming would look back at me. Like a good fairy-god cat, he was making sure I was okay.

Both of us stopped when we made it to the big wheat field, I knew we had made it to the portal. The wooden sign popped up out of the ground, fingers pointing in all directions. Each had a different school written on it pointing the way.

Eye of Newt Crystal Ball School, Tickle Palm School, Intuition

School, Wondering Wizard School, were just a few schools represented at Hidden Hall. I had attended Intuition School when I first found out about my lineage.

"Which way today?" I asked Mr. Prince Charming. No matter what finger I touched, they all led to the University and my aunt, only a different path.

Mr. Prince Charming dotted his tail in the air, pointing to Intuition School.

"Good choice." I smiled and gently ran my finger across the words. Like magic, a clear path unfolded in front of my eyes. At the end of the path, I could clearly see a small yellow cottage with geraniums, morning glories, petunias, moon flowers, and trailing ivy, a rainbow of colorful explosion in the window boxes under each window. There was a sunny, cheerfulness in my walk to where I was almost running. It felt like another extension of home.

Mr. Prince Charming was a different story. He and my aunt hadn't really seen eye-to-eye all of these years. I had never really gotten to the bottom of it, but I tried to keep the peace the best I could.

"Narley!" A voice called from ahead.

I didn't even have to look up to see who had greeted us.

Mr. Prince Charming was already in Gus Chatham's arms. Gus was a spiritual phenomenon as a teletransporter and clairvoyant medium. Though his shaggy ash-blond surfer-dude hair, brown eyes, lanky six-foot frame and his laid back cargo shirts and tee made him look like a bum.

"Hey!" I waved over my hand and picked up the pace. "How are you?"

We gave a quick hug; Mr. Prince Charming jumped out of the way and did figure eights around Gus's ankles.

"Dudette." He grabbed my hand and looked at my ring. "So the getting hitched rumor is true? Our little June is getting married."

"I guess." I eased my hand out of his and held it out to see it better.

Oscar had proposed using my mother's ring. Every time I looked at it, I saw my mother's hand. We had the exact same hands. Same bumps, same veins, same coloring.

"Oscar is kinda rushing things."

"Uh, oh. That doesn't sound so good." Gus was good at getting to the point. "Tell me about it over a cup of coffee from Black Magic."

"I would but I've got to see Aunt Helena." Though I wouldn't mind taking a stroll through the center of the University where all the shops and café were located.

"You'll have to deal with me for a while. She's in a chamber meeting with the teachers. Summer meeting thing." He shrugged. "That's why I'm here to greet you. I saw the path open and I figured it might be you."

"I guess I will have that coffee."

"See you there." Gus disappeared just like that.

"It must be nice being able to teletransport." My brow cocked as I looked at Mr. Prince Charming who was already running past the yellow cottage into the center of the University.

The street was a lot less crowded than it had been last time I was here. Granted it was summer and most spiritualists had gone home for the summer, but there was still summer school.

Black Magic Café was a really cool green clapboard house with picnic tables scattered throughout the place, providing plenty of seating.

"Hey, June!" The young guy behind the counter waved and hollered as soon as I walked in. "Gus said you were on your way. Look here." He pointed to the large chalkboard hanging on the wall behind the counter. "June's Gems!"

"Oh my gosh," I gushed when I saw the delicious dessert Raven Mortimer had named after me.

June's Gems were her version of Ding Dongs, my weakness.

"We were excited to get a deal going with her. She provides us with a lot of the cupcakes too." He pointed down the row of cupcakes.

"Wicked Good is wicked good," I laughed. "I'll definitely have a June's Gem with a cup of coffee."

"Coming up! And I'll bring it over." He gestured over to a picnic table where Gus was already sitting with Tilly, a girl who worked at Wands, Potions, and Beyond.

It was a store where any student, no matter what gift they had, could get whatever they needed while attending the University.

Tilly and I had started off on the wrong foot when I was going to school here. In fact, she was on Raven's side. They were Dark-Sider spiritualists. The Dark-Siders and Good-Siders had clearly defined lines. If prompted, Dark-Siders could pull off spells that were not for the common good and mostly didn't regret it. Times have changed and so had the Dark-Siders' point of view. I liked to think I had a hand in it since I did help create peace between the two groups, bringing me, Tilly and Raven closer as friends.

"I hear congratulations are in order!" Tilly was sitting next to Gus. She clapped in excitement. Her nails were still painted with black tips and her hair was just as purple as the day I had first met her.

"Yes, it's true. I'm getting married." I tried not to be so cheesy and smile so big, but I still couldn't believe that I was actually going to marry the man of my dreams.

"That is wonderful. I hope we are all invited." Tilly's mood was buoyant.

"Of course." My mind reeled. I hadn't even thought that far ahead. I was definitely going to have to get a jump on these things. I swallowed hard as fear and uncertainty filled my heart.

"Are you okay?" Tilly asked.

"I'm fine." I shrugged it off. "I just wish my mom was here to help me with all this stuff."

"Oh." Tilly and Gus both looked as though they didn't know what to say.

"It's okay. I have my aunt and Oscar's aunt." I guess I was glad I had them since Oscar and I were in the same boat, parent-wise. Neither of us had brought up the fact that neither set of parents was going to see us get married.

"Here you go." The guy behind the counter walked over with a tray full of goodies. "Two red velvet cupcakes and a large glass of milk for you." He slid them in front of Gus. "A June's Gem and coffee for you two."

We sat in silence, stuffing our faces with the sugary treats and burst out in laughter when we realized we probably looked like a bunch of pigs around the picnic table.

"You have white frosting on your teeth." I pointed to Gus, falling over laughing.

He licked his teeth and gritted them toward me. "Better?"

"Yes." I gasped, holding my hands across my stomach.

"Niece." Aunt Helena stood over us. Her face drew, cheeks sucked in. Her eyes held a glint of wonder, though dare she ask.

She had on her typical black outfit with red pointy boots. She wasn't one for tom-foolery. Her face was stern.

"Aunt Helena!" I jumped up and put my arms around her, feeling her thaw a bit. "I was just saying how much I need your help in planning this wedding. I came to invite you to Eloise's house for dinner."

"Dinner?" she questioned.

"Eloise is having us over to talk about the wedding." I put my hands together in the prayer position. "I really need you there. I need your help."

"This doesn't have to do with the little snafu at the factory today?" Her flat, unspeaking eyes prolonged the moment.

"Oh." My voice was a very faint whisper. "We can talk about that tonight too."

"Yes we will," she informed me matter-of-factly. "I'll be there."

"Great." I sucked in a deep breath. Something in my gut told me that more than just the two of us realized my little adventure at Head To Toe Works wasn't going as smoothly as I had promised.

After a few more minutes of catching up with Tilly and Gus, Mr. Prince Charming and I were on our way back to Whispering Falls. The day was quickly getting away from me and I still had to go back to Locust Grove to put a spell on all of bottles Burt Rossen had refused to get rid of.

CHAPTER SEVEN

There was no sense in going back through the woods to my cottage before going to Eloise's house. She lived in the woods and a hop and skip away from the wheat field.

Her house was away from Whispering Falls because of the old village rules of the segregation of the Dark-Siders from the Good-Siders.

Eloise was a Dark-Sider, but with a Good-Sider heart. I'll never forget the first time I had seen Eloise's name. It was when I had first discovered Whispering Falls. Darla had kept a journal of sorts for all of her herbal remedies, and it wasn't until I accepted I was a spiritualist that I could really read between the lines of the journal and see and understand what was there. The journal was really a potion book kept safe by Darla. Since she wasn't a spiritualist, she wasn't able to read all the potions and that was why she only did the basic homeopathic cures. . .cures without the magic. Truth be told, Darla had opened her shop in Whispering Falls when I was a baby. She would make the homeopathic cures and let Eloise stick the magic in them. According to Darla's journal, my father, Otto had become furious with her because of the Dark-Sider stamp on Eloise's forehead.

Darla had written in the journal and one entry in particular talked about her friendship with Eloise and how they had told each other their deepest and darkest secrets. When I first asked Izzy about Eloise and where I could find her, she played it off like Eloise was not a major part of my life and told me Darla didn't know her.

I knew if Darla had written about Eloise, then Eloise had to have been a big part of our lives in Whispering Falls, even if I was a baby and didn't remember it.

I was right. Eloise was magical on the day she had come to me. Her emerald eyes glowed. Beautiful fireflies surrounded her and her red hair burned bright like the sunset. She was gorgeous. And I could see where Oscar had gotten his good looks after we had discovered his relationship with her.

Needless to say, Eloise was not a dark spirit, only her lineage. She helped Whispering Falls every day. But she loved her oasis built between two trees in the woods and I didn't blame her.

Mr. Prince Charming darted up the wooden stairs that led up Eloise's two-story house with the cozy wrap-around porch. There weren't any lights on, which told me Eloise was probably tending her garden where she grew all of her incense on her own. Plus it was nice and quiet out there.

I walked around the side of her house and Mr Prince Charming stayed on the porch. The lanterns hung from the trees leading me to the gravel pathway which led to the back of her house and enchanted garden. I always enjoyed it here. There were beautiful flowers planted on both sides of the pathway. I ran my hand along the vibrant purple, green, red, orange, and yellow flowers. I couldn't help but smile when I saw the wisteria vine canopy over my head. It was the same type growing on the pergola at A Charming Cure since Eloise had helped Darla grow it.

The sweet humming voice of Eloise's I loved drifted through the air. My heart leapt and my soul filled with overwhelming joy, bringing a smile to my face when my eyes took in the rows and rows of herbs in her garden before me.

Out of nowhere, Mr. Prince Charming dove and disappeared into the honeyswell clover. Only his tail danced happily above the magical herb. It was like catnip to him and he loved it.

At the beginning of each herb row was a small wooden sign where Eloise had painted the name. Rose petals, moonflower, mandrake root, seaweed, shrinking violet, dream dust, fairy dust, magic peanut, lucky clover, steal rose, spooky shroom were just a few that I held so dearly to my heart. Each of these had somehow played a little part in my potion making. They also played a little part in someone's life outside of our magical village.

In the distance, nearer to the house, the twinkling lights strung around the gazebo shone down on a table that was set for four. Eloise must've gotten wind that Aunt Helena was coming.

"Hello." Eloise called out from underneath the singing nettles. "I'll be done in a minute."

The singing flowering plant hummed right along with her. She stood up and used her fingers like a conductor's stick. "Hmmmm," she held the hum for a few seconds to get them geared up.

I stood silently with my hands clasped in front of me to watch the show.

"Laaaaleeeee." A happy tune came from Eloise's mouth. Her brows lifted, her cheeks drew in and her fingers slowly swayed over the singing nettles.

"Laaaaaleeee," the nettles repeated in harmony.

"Leeeeelaaaaalooooo," Eloise's sweet voice filled the vacant space and the singing nettles chimed in. Each growing a tad bit more as they continued with the harmony. "Leeeelooooleeeelaaaa," the entire group harmonized while Eloise's pointer fingers swayed to the music. Her eyes were closed and her head swept side-to-side in a fluid motion.

I closed my eyes and sucked in a deep breath, letting the sounds of the nettles and the aromas of the herb garden fill my insides. It was like a cleansing to my spiritual soul.

Magic boiled inside my veins as little shocks of lightning jumped inside me, making me blissfully happy, fully alive, and leaving my heart singing with delight.

Marrying Oscar had to be top on my list. Deep in my intuition, I knew this was the right place to be and this was my top priority, not some big national store and stress free lotion.

"This is a double-day leaf." Eloise lifted a long, thick leaf up in the air. It hummed out in delight. "I've been trying to come up with something for baby Orin. Goodness gracious, Petunia won't give that baby a pacifier. If she keeps feeding him, he's going to be as big as a house."

"So this is a singing pacifier?" I asked and studied it.

"It sure is." She brought it back down and looked at it. She smiled. "Petunia is going to love it because it's natural and not bad for baby Orin like she thinks sucking on plastic is. And when you and Oscar have babies, I'll be ready."

"Don't fall for it," a husky voice broke the sweet melody floating through the air. "She just wants to make sure that everyone gets what is coming to them with this union." Aunt Helena's icy eyes flashed a gentle yet firm warning my way.

"Oh get off your high horse and let these two finally be together like it's written in the spiritual stars." Eloise's emerald eye pierced the space between the two dueling aunts.

"I was afraid this was going to happen," Aunt Helena swept across the garden as though she were floating on air. "That is why I brought a mediator."

"Gus?" I questioned when Gus had teletransported near the drowsy moon flowers.

He picked one up and held it up to his nose before he stuck it in his mouth and ate it.

"Mmmmm," he licked his lips. "Very delicious Eloise."

"Oh, Gus." Eloise crossed over the rows of herbs and took Gus into her arms. "Helena, you can't possibly think this child could be an observer of such a union."

"Union?" I laughed thinking these two were ridiculous. "Oscar and I are simply getting married. That's all."

Rowlll! Mr. Prince Charming curled up on the tips of his claws and howled up to the sky.

"Have you all gone mad?" I plunged on carelessly, "Oscar and I are just two people getting married. Two people in love. Childhood friends that found happiness."

"June, dear." Eloise flew to my side.

"My June dear." Aunt Helena nearly knocked Eloise over trying to get closer to me. "Your mother and father," she started.

"And Oscar's mother and father. . ." Eloise gulped.

"Had our marriage arranged." Oscar stood underneath the pergola with the last bit of the day's sun glowing like a flashlight around him.

His gaze traveled over my face and searched my eyes as if I knew something.

Then it hit me.

Oscar had known all along that we were bound by a prearranged marriage and not destined to fall in love as I had thought.

"Why do you think she hasn't answered either of you when you tell her to plan a date?" Aunt Helena turned toward me. A spark flew from her eyes. "Your intuition is right. You cannot get married when the sun is not transitioning between Taurus and Libra. You know that."

"That is by your calendar." Eloise tsked, referring to how the Good-Siders tend to use the astrological calendar on the timing of things. "According to ours, the moon is almost in prime position for a partnership event." She gestured between Oscar and I. "Like the marriage of two people in love."

"Calendar, moon." I shook my head. "Who cares! You all have ruined this for me!"

"June! June!" Oscar yelled out into the night air. There was no sense in me hanging around and listening to them argue. Nothing was going to get solved.

The moonlight dotted the ground leading my path out of the woods. I didn't have to stand there and listen to the three of them go on and on about how much Oscar loved me and that no matter if there was an agreement or not, our lives were destined to be one.

I knew that. I knew that from my intuition churning inside. But it was still hard to hear and made me mad to think about it.

"June." Oscar caught up to me and grabbed me by my arm.

Hiss, hiss. Mr. Prince Charming stood up on two legs and batted his paws at Oscar, claws out.

Mr. Prince Charming had always had a jealous nature about him when it came to Oscar. Before I knew I was a spiritualist, I thought Mr. Prince Charming was just wanting my time instead of hanging out under the big oak tree in Oscar's front yard eating Ding Dongs and any other junk food Oscar's uncle kept in the house since Darla never let me eat any thing unhealthy or sugary, unless it had a manager's special sticker on it.

After I found out Mr. Prince Charming was my familiar fairy-god cat, I knew he was only trying to protect me like he was now. Only I didn't need protecting from Oscar.

"Mr. Prince Charming," I scolded and drew my eyes back toward Oscar.

He had changed out of his Whispering Falls police uniform into a pair of baggy jeans and form-fitting white tee shirt. He took my bag from around my shoulder and set it on the ground.

Oscar's eyes searched mine for answers I was holding deep down; only I didn't even know what those answers were.

"I love you. You know I love you. Arrangement or not." Oscar's large hand took my face and held it gently. "We can move away from here and try to live a normal life like my parents. I don't care."

"That wouldn't solve anything." A brief shiver ripped through me, sending my intuition on high alert. "But Aunt Helena is right."

There was no way I was going to start a marriage off on a bad feeling. It was hard enough trying to turn off my internal witchy side and live in the world around us, but I just couldn't ignore the strange feeling brewing inside of me.

"We can do whatever it is you want." He gathered me into his arms, snuggling me tightly. "I'm not a Dark-Sider like Eloise. I'm just plain old Oscar Park from Locust Grove, Kentucky who happened to fall madly, deeply in love with his childhood neighbor June Heal."

"And when did you just so happen to fall in love?" I giggled, feeling a little safer in his arms. The wind whipped and I nuzzled my head deeper into his chest.

"The day I got the call from Mac McGurtle about you blowing up your shed." His lips pressed into the top of my head. Slowly he put his hand on my chin and lifted my face up. He moved his arms to wrap around my midriff and cuffed his hands on the small of my back. "I've never looked back. Through all the good, the bad, my memory loss. Nothing."

The touch of his lips on mine was a delicious sensation.

"Please don't stop." I smiled from ear-to-ear longing to have his warmth embrace around me.

"I've got to work the night shift in Locust Grove tonight." As he talked, my eyes froze on the softness of his lips. "I was hoping to have a nice quiet dinner under Eloise's gazebo and discuss your first day at Head To Toe Works."

"Well, I have to go back tomorrow." I snuggled a little closer knowing my time was limited. "There was a bit of a mix up."

"Like what?" He pulled away to look at me. His eyes shone bright in the pale light of the moon as it was peeking out for the night.

"Nothing for you to worry about." I shirked it off. If Oscar knew what I was going to do tonight, he would tell me to forget it. He'd tell me that it's only a couple hundred bottles—where I seen it as a couple hundred people I could help. "I will see you bright and early tomorrow."

"And we can discuss the wedding later." His words put comfort back in my heart. I knew I was going to be Mrs. Oscar Park, I just didn't know when. I was going to have to rely on my witchy senses to tell me.

CHAPTER EIGHT

I knew this wedding was going to be a big deal and if there were a way around it, I would do it. I was envious of the couples that could do a destination wedding by going off to some exotic island or the couple who could simply go to the Justice of the Peace and get married in a small room at the courthouse.

Not in the spiritual community.

Weddings were a big deal. Especially when two spiritualists come together. Petunia and Gerald had showed me how big their wedding was and I wasn't looking forward to it.

Since my parents weren't here, I knew Aunt Helena was going to make sure it was done the Heal way and that included the spiritual side of events.

"June." Aunt Helena sat at my kitchen table when I got home after saying my goodnight to Oscar. "I had to come straightaway." She stood up and unfurled her arms. The sleeves of her cloak hung nearly to the ground. "Come."

"No. I'm fine." Her voice was bland. "I'm not a pawn in this little game between you and Eloise."

"It's not a game." The words dripped out of her mouth as if she really meant them. Only I knew better. "You are my only remaining niece and

I have to see to it that you have the wedding of your dreams. A proper wedding that includes all the Order of Elders, all the Presidents of all the villages, all the dignitaries throughout the different colleges, and the teachers. . ."

She rambled on and on about all the fancy people who I didn't know but I let her and took out Madame Torres.

The globe glowed fiery red. Streaks of purple and yellow burst throughout the glass in little waves of lightning. Madame Torres appeared. The lime green turban propped on the top of her head. Her eyes grew large and liquid, melting into a wavy scene playing out at Head To Toe Works headquarters in the factory near the new conveyor belt. As the scene played out, it showed Burt in some sort of argument with someone—a shadowy figure. The person's back was to me but one of my bottles was visible in the clutches of the person's fisted hand and another in Burt's hand.

I grabbed the globe and put it back into my bag.

"Aunt Helena, you must go." I reached my arms out to the side and created a big fake yawn. "I'm tired and we can talk about this in a couple of days." I pointed to the clock. "Look at the time. It's late and I have to work tomorrow."

"We all work tomorrow." Her brow cocked as she watched me suspiciously. "The wedding isn't causing all of your strange behavior. What is really going on with you?"

"Nothing." I opened the door and secretly thanked the world for the spiritual laws. Rule Number One in particular. It deemed that no other spiritualist could read another spiritualist. Meaning Aunt Helena couldn't try to figure out what was really bothering me.

Those bottles and me getting there to put a spell on them.

"No need for a door." She crossed her arms around her and in a blink of an eye and a puff of blue smoke, she was gone.

I took Madame Torres back out of the bag.

"Tell me who seeks me." I gave her a specific order. Could the shadowy figure have been Tiffany and there was an argument between her and Burt about me, otherwise they wouldn't have been holding the bottles.

Madame Torres's globe stayed black.

I set her on the kitchen table and with a loud voice demanded, "Show me Head To Toe Works Headquarters."

"I tried earlier," Madame Torres spoke with an attitude. "*Phewt, phewt*. Wasn't important to you then so it must not be important now." Her face rippled as it floated inside the liquid globe.

"Are we really going to have to go through an argument?" I planted my hands on my hips. "I'm in no way, shape or form wanting to worry with you. I will throw you in the bottom of my bag until further notice." Nothing happened. Her ball stayed black. "Or I can drop you off at the Locust Grove Flea Market tomorrow and let someone else take you home."

"You wouldn't dare!" She appeared. She glared at me with a burning, reproachful eye.

"Oh, I would." I knew that one would get her goat.

She was my crystal ball and she was created specifically for me. If she was taken or given to someone else, she would spend the rest of her life suspended in the unknown and simply be a snow globe.

"Fine!" She spat and showed me the inside of the headquarters, sort of like a virtual tour.

There was nothing there and everyone had seemed to go home, even Burt and Tiffany. I was sure I would hear about their spat in the morning during one of our meetings, but for now, there was one thing for certain. No one was there and it was my signal to drive over there and put the spell on those few hundred bottles before they were shipped out.

CHAPTER NINE

The Head To Toe Works shopping bag with my uniform was still on the floorboard of the Green Machine. I wasn't looking forward to wearing the outfit tomorrow, nor was I looking forward to putting the little extra oomph in all of those plastic bottles tonight.

The security station had a faint light on and when I pulled up, I noticed a different security guard from this morning. It wasn't Ronald. Too bad I couldn't just get through because the guy had his feet propped up on the desk, hands folded, and hat over top of his eyes.

I beeped the Green Machine's horn and he nearly fell out of his chair. He slid the window open and I rolled mine down.

"They are closed." He cleared his throat.

"I work here. I'm June Heal, the new employee. Ronald knows me." I smiled happily.

"They aren't open at nights. There is no reason you should be here." He didn't budge.

"I have to get a new size for my uniform in the morning." I grabbed the bag off the floor and held it up. "You know how Tiffany and Burt can be if things aren't just right." I laughed nervously and used my other finger to make the crazy sign around my ear.

He harrumphed and tilted his head down to look further in my car.

"Is that a cat? A real cat?" He flicked on his flashlight and shone it on Mr. Prince Charming curled up on the dash.

"Yes." I planted another smile on my face. "Can you please let me in?" I thought asking nicely might help, but I was losing my patience.

"No can do." He stood back up and placed the tips of his thumbs in the belt around his waist. "Sorry. You'll have to see Mrs. Rossen in the morning."

He slid the window shut and took his seat back in the chair.

"This is when I wish I had Gus's gift," I whined and put the car in reverse. It didn't bother Mr. Prince Charming any.

When I looked back to go in reverse, my bag was glowing. I pulled out of the Head To Toe Works headquarters and pulled off on the side of the road.

"What's up?' I asked Madame Torres after I pulled her out of the bag.

"There is an open entrance on the loading dock if you can get in there." She was actually trying to be helpful. "But you must first smudge the area from which you seek."

"Oh crap." I had totally forgotten to try to smudge the plant like Eloise had told me to do. "I'll do that. But how am I going to get in?"

"That's for you to figure out." Madame Torres's face took up the entire globe. "I'm just here to give general information."

I took a deep breath to keep me from saying anything mean. When I had been mean to her before, she would just shut off and pout.

"Technically since I didn't start today, the smudging should be fine." I was really regretting that I didn't somehow get to smudge Head To Toe Works headquarters. I thought back to the little time I was in there, I'd been surrounded by so many people that there was no time.

Slowly, I drove around the fortress of the headquarters. There was a brick wall all the way around with barbed wire on top. There were trees planted in front of the wall as if it were to make the wall look better.

I parked the car a fair distance away from the security gate entrance between two trees on the side of the road. The Green Machine would be covered by the shadows the moon had created from the trees and no one would see my car.

"Come on." I leaned back in the seat and looked at my ornery cat.

He simply yawned, stretched his front paws out in front of him and put his head back down.

"I guess I'm going in alone?" I asked as though he was going to answer me. He didn't budge. I grabbed Madame Torres and stuck her in my bag. "She's going with me."

There was one thing I didn't like. Being in the dark alone. Alone in the dark in a big building was even more terrifying. I ran my hand over my charm bracelet and said, "Anything that was sent to harm me, I turn into my good." I grabbed my kit of homemade goodies.

I left the car windows open halfway for Mr. Prince Charming and darted across the street when I felt like the coast was clear. Who was I kidding? It was well past ten o'clock at night and no one left their houses after nine in Locust Grove. The headquarters were so far out of town; no one would be driving these roads at night.

It was easy to walk behind the trees and trace along the brick wall. Every once in a while I would glance up at the barbed wire to see if there was a break. Finally, there was. It wasn't the best break, but it looked like the end of one wire and they had to add new, so it wasn't exactly matching, making the break a little less prickly.

I shimmied up the tree (luckily I was good at it since Oscar was my childhood best friend and he was always climbing trees) and propelled myself on the top of the wall. Carefully I jumped over the barbed wire and landed on the other side. If only my cat was here because he would've been proud of me landing on my feet.

Madame Torres was right. Off in the distance, butted up to the back of the building, were several eighteen-wheel trucks that I was sure were ready for tomorrow morning's shipments to go out.

There wasn't any movement, so I decided to run over by staying in the shadows of the night. When I heard some voices, I planted my back up against the building and slid my way down until I could get a good look at who was there.

There were two more security guards outside on the steps leading from the building smoking. After they put out their cigarettes, I heard one say he was going to keep the door propped open so not to put the alarm back on.

After giving them a few minutes to get back inside, I decided to make my move. With my bag across my body, Madame Torres deep inside, and my kit in my grip, I kept my hand around my other wrist to make sure my charm bracelet was there and headed inside.

"Show me the security guards," I said to Madame Torres once I felt like I could safely pull her out after I found small space in the warehouse.

Her ball whirled and twirled like a tornado until it calmed. The men were in a room where they were eating and drinking while watching the late show on the TV.

"I guess that will occupy them for a while." I stuck her back in my bag and found my way up to the front of the building where Tiffany had brought me in this morning.

I put the kit on top of the counter where Tiffany had gotten my clothes from and opened it. I took out the smudge stick Eloise had given me and used my matches to light it.

"Air, fire, water, earth. Cleanse, dismiss, dispel." The smoke moved away from me as I used the large eagle's feather to push it up and into the air as I continued to chant, "Air, fire, water, earth. Cleanse, dismiss, dispel."

It was a basic cleanse for the space I was going to occupy. There was always some type of bad karma in buildings but if I was going to work there, I needed all the bad ju-ju to go away and this wasn't going to hurt.

I traced the path Tiffany and I had walked since I knew I would probably be working within those areas. Since I wasn't sure how to get to my office from where I was, I left that for now, but I knew I would be on the line, keeping a close eye on my product, so I headed there.

Slowly I walked down the stairs, fanning the smoke as evenly as I possibly could so it would form a barrier over the co-packing part of the plant. I was happy to see the new belt for the bottles I had chosen was moving, but wondered who was running it.

The thought crossed my mind that Tiffany had someone stay longer to get the product started, but my bottles were still in the boxes I had sent them in and the cheap plastic bottles were packaged and ready to go.

There was no way I was going to bother with stopping the new belt because I had no idea what I was doing, and no one was around. I put the smudge stick out, happy with my progress and walked over to the packaged bottles Burt had okayed for my stress free line and opened it.

"Gross." I took out one of the plastic bottles. The cheap container really did dull the product making me more stressed. With my other hand, I took out Madame Torres and set her on the ground and I took a seat next to her. "I'm going to need your energy." I told her and held the bottle in my grip and lifted it up into the smoky room. "Any stress that you hold must go. From inside out and outside in, stress be gone while rubbing in."

I sucked in a deep breath and let the energy run through my fingers that Madame Torres was giving me. I wasn't able to cast many spells but with the help of my smudging and intuitive gift, I was able to do some.

One by one, Madame Torres and I held each bottle up, saying the same thing over.

"Last one." I was so tired of chanting. I had no idea what time it was, but I was sure by the time I made it back to Whispering Falls, I was going to have to turn around and come back. But it was worth it. Each product that Burt insisted had to go out needed to go out with the intention.

"What in the hell are you doing in here?" One of the security guys fanned his hand in front of his face. "Who are you?" His eyes slid over to the still moving belt with nothing on it.

"Hi, I'm June. I work here. I'm sure if you call Tiffany Rossen, she'll say it's okay I'm here." I stood up and tried to hide Madame Torres from being seen.

"What's all this smoke? And why is the machine running?" He kept his hand on his security belt. Though he didn't have a gun, he had a billy club. He walked over to the machine and smacked a couple of the buttons on the side like Tiffany had done this morning.

Rowl! Mr. Prince Charming jumped on top of the machine, whacking the button with his tail, starting the belt again.

The machine made the awful screeching sound setting the conveyor belt in motion. Both the security guard and myself covered our ears. We watched as the belt slowly came to a stop. Sticking out from underneath the flaps where the finished product rolled out was not a Gentle June Stress Free Lotion bottle, but a pair of shoes, attached to feet, and attached to legs and attached to one dead Burt Rossen.

"The black butterfly," I gasped, remembering how the symbol of death had floated out of Petunia Shrubwood's hair as she stood in A Charming Cure.

CHAPTER TEN

"I swear I don't know anything about it." I bit my lip and glanced over Oscar's shoulder to get a better look at the dead body of Burt Rossen. Someone had shot him dead.

"All I know is that woman was over there doing some sort of voodoo crap in the corner with that snow globe glowing and this place with filled with smoke. Lots of smoke." The security guard's fat finger was pointing at me.

"I was not doing voodoo." I had to shut that train of thought down quickly. The last thing I needed was any type of rumors running around about me, though he was sort of right. "I'm the owner of this product and I wanted to make sure all the bottles were completely filled before they were shipped."

"And you were in here with that, that, and him." He pointed to Madame Torres, Mr. Prince Charming who was too busy cleaning himself to help me out. . .some fairy-god cat. And he gestured to the dead body. "I came in here, cleared the smoke and shut down the machine." The guard took his hat off and shook his head. He leaned in and whispered more toward Oscar's way, "I don't know how that cat did it, but he jumped up on the machine and hit the on button with his tail. If it weren't for him, this woman would've left and Mr. Rossen,

God bless his soul, wouldn't have been found until Pearl started her shift."

"Pearl? Pearl!" I snapped my fingers. My intuition told me Pearl was the name of the woman I had met this morning and who really wanted my bottles to be used and not the cheap ones. "Yes. Pearl would know me."

"Then I called the sheriff's department with this baby pointed at her the whole time." The security guard patted the billy club on his belt. "She tried to talk her way out of this, but I know a witch when I see one."

"Witch?" Oscar's eyes drew. "You believe in witches?"

"Hell, no, but I've seen plenty of people do some weirdo things and she was doing some weirdo things." The guard's mouth pinched as did his eyes when he looked my way.

"Did you see this woman pick up Mr. Rossen and put him on the conveyor belt?" Oscar asked. The man shook his head. "Did you see her knock him on the head with whatever blunt object caused the gash on his head?"

"Um . . .no." As the coroner rolled Burt Rossen's body, the guard watched, his face flushed, turning white.

"Then I'd say leave all the speculation to the sheriff's department." Oscar nodded and excused himself, tugging on the sleeve of my shirt to follow him.

In the corner of the packing room, Oscar decided to question me.

"What in the world are you doing here?" His eyes held a questioning stare. He was able to drown out the world around us, but I wasn't.

"I was going to tell you earlier, but then the whole wedding thing." I rolled my eyes.

"What are you doing here?" His voice more demanding this time.

"Burt had decided, against my contract, that he was going to use a different bottle than the ones I had sent." I lifted my brows and slowly moved my head forward.

"The magic is in the bottles?" Oscar had never really asked how I got the magic in the new line for Head To Toe Works and it was an unspoken rule not to question how another spiritualist used their gift.

"Yes." I sucked in a deep breath and tucked a strand of hair behind my ear. "That is how the stress free lotion will work. The lotion is all the homeopathic herbs, but when the recipient touches my bottle, not the fake plastic one, their touch activates the right ingredient they need for their specific stress."

"Burt didn't use your bottles?" He was putting two and two together.

"When I came in to work this morning, they had these bottles going through the assembly line, squirting my lotion into them. I refused to let them continue to bottle my lotion in the cheap non-magical bottles." My head jerked when I heard the shriek of Tiffany Rossen.

She was standing in the window overlooking the assembly line floor with the palms of her hands planted up against the glass. Her palms fisted and she screamed inaudible words while banging the glass.

Over my dead body. Her words from earlier floated around in my head. *Burt is not in charge of my company.* I recalled her angry words from when Ronald had refused to let me in. And why wasn't I on the list? Did Burt deliberately leave me off because of the bottles? What about that security guard? He was quick to blame me. Did he know more than he was letting on?

My wrist felt warm and I glanced down at my charm bracelet. The liquid in the little potion bottle was bubbling again. I rubbed it with my other hand.

"June," Oscar spit my name out in a hushed whisper, "I asked you a question."

"I'm sorry. What did you ask?" I looked back up at Tiffany where she was on the floor completely in grief. There was a woman bending down next to her.

"First off, did you get the magic in the plastic bottles?" Oscar was so cute trying to make sure our deal with Head To Toe Works went exactly as I had told them it would.

"Yes." I leaned over and whispered so no one would hear me. "Unfortunately, the guard did see me smudging."

"Smudging? I thought Aunt Eloise told you to do that this morning. First thing." His face was a glowing mask of rage. I didn't have to say anything for him to read my face. "And you wonder why he called you a voodoo witch." Oscar ran his hands through his hair. "When are you going to learn to listen to our elders?"

"I don't know." I shrugged.

A veil of grey cloud hovered over the conveyor belt of the assembly line. Three faces appeared in the haze. My gut dropped. It was bad enough that Burt was found dead in the mortal world, but seeing The Order of Elders here was another thing, making an even more terrifying realization wash over me.

"Why are they here?" I swallowed hard, trying to manage the answer to my own question.

It was never a good thing when the Marys, the Elders, showed up.

"Oh no." His expression stilled and grew serious. "Don't say a word here. Do you understand me? People are watching."

I did what he said and just nodded my head.

CHAPTER ELEVEN

"Oh, June! I told you to smudge first thing." Eloise wrung her hands together. The hem of her cloak swished against the hardwood floors of Full Moon Treesort. "I even heard Petunia had a black butterfly fall out of her hair. That was sign enough that you needed to smudge."

Full Moon Treesort was big enough for everyone to gather in the only hotel sort of shop in Whispering Falls. Full Moon Treesort had all the fine luxuries of the fanciest hotels in the world. It was owned and operated by Amethyst Plum. Her spiritual gift of Onerirocriticy (dream interpretations), perfectly fit with her being the owner of Full Moon.

She was able to tell when one of her guests was having a dream, good or bad, and alter their stay to make it very enjoyable.

"I was afraid my dream was going to come true." Amethyst pushed her long black curly hair behind her shoulders and drummed her fingers together. She stood behind the bar top in the kitchen.

I sat on one of the barstools along with Gerald, Izzy, and Chandra. Petunia was in one of the comfy chairs near the fireplace, nestling baby Orin in her arms. The Marys were huddled in the corner as though they were having a meeting.

Mary Lynn stood in the middle of them and they were bent down to accommodate her four-foot tall frame. She wore a black dress that hung down to the top of her black pointy laced-up witch shoes. Her tight silvery hair was tucked under a small black pillbox hat with lace hanging around the edges. There was a fox stole wrapped around her shoulders and clipped on by the teeth of the creature. Only it wasn't dead.

She ran her hands down the fur and snapped her fingers. The fox uncurled off her neck and jumped down, finding a hook on the coat rack across the room. Mr. Prince Charming lifted his head off the hearth of the fireplace and watched.

Mary Ellen was much younger than the other two Marys and the most stylish. She wore a one-piece bright red jumper and cheetah print high heels.

Mary Sue was what Mary Ellen called the "old coot" of the Marys. She was the typical witch type that wore the long sleeved black dress, the pointy black hat, and black lace up boots. She really did take her job seriously. She was the most brash of the three and her deep voice made me take notice when she talked.

"What dream?" I asked Amethyst.

Her eyes darted between me and the three Marys. She leaned on the bar top on her elbows. "When Tiffany and Burt stayed here during Christmas, Tiffany had a dream that Burt died. Of course I didn't say anything because I was afraid my dream was off due to the stress Tiffany caused me with her complaints. I was having a hard time distinguishing if it was her dream or my dream to implicate her in some way. After they were snowed in a few nights, the dream was more vivid than ever."

"Is that why you told me to have June smudge the headquarters?" Eloise asked her.

"And shouldn't I have know about this?" My mouth dropped. "This would've been some pretty important information."

"After you had given Tiffany the stress relief, the dream didn't occur anymore. So I figured everything was working out and there was no need to step in." Her eyes drew up and stared at me. Her long flashes created a shadow on her cheeks. "Do you remember the soup I had made for the guests with Eloise's organic vegetables?"

"I do and it was delicious." I recalled how Tiffany had complained about Full Moon and how she didn't think Amethyst was using organic vegetables. I had gone to Eloise and asked her to donate some veggies to the Full Moon and she had.

"I had a special spell to put in there to help fix her dream of the death of her husband, but the dreams stopped." Amethyst pushed herself back up on her feet and took the dishcloth, wiping down the counter.

The coffee pot had brewed and she took five cups off the hooks on the wall and filled them up with the brew. One by one, she went down the counter setting a cup in front of each of us.

Izzy, Gerald, and Chandra kept to themselves. They were on edge because they were waiting on the Marys to make a decision on what we as a village should do. Petunia continued to care for baby Orin. Since she was the village president, the Marys would go to her first, and then they would call a meeting at The Gathering Rock for the others to join.

"I didn't get her stress wrong, did I?" I asked with doubt in my head.

Tiffany was so stressed out about Christmas and making deviled eggs of all things. Burt's mother was a stickler for the eggs and since Tiffany was hosting the family dinner, she knew his mother would complain if they weren't just right. I gave her the stress free potion to help her get through and not worry about the eggs. She said it had worked and that was how I got the deal at Head To Toe Works.

"Oh no, she had stress about those darn eggs," Amethyst's eyes were compelling, magnetic, drawing me into her dream. "Her dream really captivated her heart. With each stir of those egg yellows, she envisioned stabbing Burt with the fork tines."

"Death by fork?" I made a half-witted joke to break the unnerving glare in her eyes.

"You see where it has gotten us. It has come true," her words trailed off. Her face turned to see who was coming into the room.

"Everyone." Oscar took his Locust Grove sheriff's hat off and greeted everyone, but his eyes were on me. He walked over and hugged me.

"What is this for?" I squeezed back feeling safe in his embrace.

"That could've been you," his husky voice broke. "I don't know what would've happened if you walked in a few minutes earlier."

"I swear there wasn't anyone in there. The only people I saw were the security guards." I rested my head in the crook of his neck. He pulled me away.

"Don't tell me anything else." He spoke loudly. His tone felt strange to my ear.

"By the Orders of the Elders," Mary Ellen floated above me. Her long black hair hung past her shoulders. Next to her were the other Marys. "You will not speak of this to Oscar Park since he is the official officer on duty. And we will be accompanying you to work."

"That is not a good idea." I kept one of my arms curled around Oscar's waist. "Besides, I didn't do it."

"We know that but others are going to try to accuse you of it." Mary Ellen floated down and planted her leopard print heels firmly on the ground. "And we want to be at the ready."

"I get that. I do, but how am I going to explain three floating women?" I asked.

"We aren't going to be there, be there," she explained.

"Okay." That was fine. I would be able to work around them. "Then what about Oscar?"

"I agree that you don't need to say a word until Mac gets here." Oscar referred to our village lawyer Mac McGurtle.

Mac was also my next-door neighbor in Locust Grove. As a child I just thought he was a nosy neighbor who always looked over the hedges when in reality he was keeping an eye on me for the spiritual community as I lived in the mortal world.

"I have summoned him from one of the western villages where he is helping a family transition into the mortal world." Mary Sue stood in between me and Mary Ellen. "I told him to get his a-double-s here now."

Mary Sue was the more brash and honest of the three Marys and more masculine. Her voice was raspy, harsh at times and definitely deeper.

"He did send a telegraph saying he was going to meet June tomorrow at the Head To Toe Works Headquarters for the rescheduled meeting." Petunia stood up.

Baby Orin cried out from his slumber. Petunia simply pulled one of Eloise's double-day leaves out of her messy hair and stuck it in his mouth. I wasn't sure what was worse, sucking on plastic or sucking on a leaf that had who knows what on it from being in the mop of a hair-do Petunia had. Regardless, baby Orin sucked happily and the double-day sang him back to sleep.

"What is that?" Mary Sue swept over to Petunia's side. Everyone gawked.

"A double-day." I shrugged as though everyone should know. "The alternative to a plastic binky."

"Interesting," Mary Sue continued to survey the double-day from all angles.

For a brief moment all eyes were off me. Brief as it was, it was nice to get a breath.

"Listen to them." Oscar wasn't fooling around as he warned me. "Do not go into any meetings until Mac is there."

"Promise." I sealed the deal with a kiss.

As much as I wanted to enjoy Oscar's lips on mine, I couldn't. The nagging feeling that something bad was about to happen didn't stop with the murder of Burt Rossen.

CHAPTER TWELVE

The next morning, I downed a pot of coffee and made sure I had all of my kit together including Madame Torres by my side, along with Mr. Prince Charming. Most of my night was spent in one of my nightmare dreams.

I had had them all my life and most times they had come true or helped me see visions that were to come true.

Meow, meow. Mr. Prince Charming rubbed up against me. I bent down and picked him up.

"You know." I looked at my fairy-god cat. "The dream was so real. I had gone to visit Darla and Dad's grave but it wasn't like I was there to see her. I was sitting in front of their stones and my dad was sitting next to me," my voice broke.

I sat down on the kitchen floor. Mr. Prince Charming stepped on my leg and purred.

"I barely remember my dad." Tears built up in my eyes. I gave my cat a good scratch behind the ears. I shook the idea the dream had any meaning. It wasn't like I didn't have regular dreams. Besides, I was getting married to Oscar and what girl wouldn't want her parents there? "We've got to go."

After gathering everything I needed in the Green Machine,

including Mr. Prince Charming, it took no time to get to Head To Toe Works. I had no idea what was in store for me, but I was armed and ready to face the day.

"Ronald." I pointed to my shirt to show him my uniform.

"I. . .a. . .I," he gasped for air as his mouth flopped open and shut. He slammed the glass window to the security booth and pushed the button for the gates to open. He waved me in and didn't make eye contact.

"That was easy." I drove up the long drive of the Head To Toe Works headquarters.

Mr. Prince Charming was sitting in the seat next to me. He pawed at my bag. When I came to the parking lot, I parked and dug out Madame Torres.

"Thanks, buddy." Mr. Prince Charming was a good fairy-god cat when he needed to be and Madame Torres was ablaze.

"Do not," she warned from a dark ball, "let anyone pick me up and juggle me around again. Do you understand?"

"I can't help it if they think you are pretty." I knew flattery would get me nowhere, but it was worth a shot.

"If someone does, I will not appear when you call," she threatened which didn't sit well with me so I threw her back in my bag.

"Let's do this." I stared at the building and took in a deep breath. I was going to need it. Oscar had to work on the case all night and they made sure to scour the entire building so the factory could be up and running. Out of my rear-view mirror I noticed a Head To Toe Works truck leaving the facility. On the side of the eighteen-wheeler was a big picture of Gentle June's Stress Relief with a bow across the whole truck announcing the new arrival.

There was a lot riding on this. Not just the future of Head To Toe Works, but my success as a spiritualist taking her product to the mortal world.

"So you did come back!" Pearl sat at the desk like she had yesterday. She smacked her hands together and got up from the chair. She walked over to the secretary station and pushed a few buttons before talking. "Josh, I won." Her voice echoed all over the building.

"What?" I asked. "Am I not supposed to be here?"

"Josh bet me one-hundred dollars you wouldn't come back after what happened to Mr. Rossen."

"No way, dude!" Josh flung open the door. "You are back. Far out." His lanky body bounced up and down. "I figured you were off the curve. Damn." He pulled out a wad of cash from his pocket, thumbed through it, and smacked down a Benjamin on the top of the counter.

"Nice doing business with you." Pearl cackled and stuck the one-hundred dollar bill down into her shirt. "So did you do it?" Pearl leaned over the counter. She had a hard, cold-eyed smile.

"Do what?" I drew back, a little offended.

"Off'ed the boss." Josh smirked. "Hell, we've been here for years dreaming of it. You get in a little scuffle with him and in a few hours he's dead." He ran his finger across his neck like a knife. "Or did your little friend do it? Or something else?" He wiggled his fingers in the air insinuating some sort of magic.

"Of course I didn't." My mouth dropped. "And you think I did? I'm here to save your jobs and with my product, it will happen." I turned on my heels. "Let's go, Mr. Prince Charming."

As I was leaving the front office, I could hear Pearl and Josh whispering behind my back. They had their suspicions about me and rightly so since I was new, but to think I would kill Burt.

It was true we did have a little disagreement, but there were never threats like the one Tiffany...

"It's always the wife," Pearl sputtered.

I gulped.

"Tiffany," I whispered and looked down at Mr. Prince Charming. "Do you think?"

I bit my lip and glanced around when I heard a faint buzz. The black circle on the wall had to be a security camera and they were watching me. I bent down and picked up Mr. Prince Charming and walked into my office, locking the door behind me.

I pulled out Madame Torres and sat her on the desk in front of me. I eased down in the chair and leaned back, contemplating what to ask her. Mr. Prince Charming sat in the desk next to her, his tail swaying back and forth with a flick on the desk top.

"Madame Torres, show me the fight from last night right before Burt got killed." I wanted to get a good look at the surrounding area and see if there were any other clues.

Tiffany made no bones about it. She definitely had her beef with Burt and he did grab her by the face, which was good enough reason for her to kill him, at least in my book.

The insides of Madame Torres's ball swirled purple with good flecks before parting. It was like watching a movie; she played back the scene. Burt was facing the "camera" and the shadowy figure's back was to me, finger pointing between the two conveyor belts. Burt's hand was lifted in the air with one of my potion bottles in his grip. With his other hand, he lifted it to the shadowy figure's face and grabbed it like he had done to Tiffany in front of me. Only this time he shook her head back and forth, his teeth gritted and eyes seething anger.

There had to be something to give a clue.

"Please, she..." I looked around the room instead of focusing on Burt's activities but nothing seemed to be out of the ordinary, though I had only been in there twice.

No weapons lying around. No one else in the room. Just Burt and Tiffany yelling at each other.

"Please replay," I told Madame Torres in hopes to see something one more time, this time focusing on the shadowy figure, hoping to get an idea on the size of the person to determine whether it was a woman or man. The only thing I noticed was the shadow grabbed Burt's wrist to stop his hand from reaching up for the person and that was when it cut off. "Rewind a little bit."

My eyes focused on the dark shadow's hand that had grabbed Burt. The fingers were long, thin and there were painted nails on the end. A woman.

"Tiffany," I whispered. This seemed reason enough for her to kill him. If he was grabbing her and abusing her, surely it was an act of trying to save herself.

"June?" The knock at the door caused me to jump. It was Tiffany on the other side. "June? Can you open the door?"

I hurried and put Madame Torres on the edge of the desk like she was a decoration and shoo'ed Mr. Prince Charming off the top of the desk before I walked over to the door to let her in.

"Tiffany, how are you this morning?" I asked noticing there wasn't a hair on her head out of place. She had on a hot pink shirt with the Head To Toe Works logo in black and pink pants. The opposite of what she made the employees wear. A pair of large black sunglasses covered her eyes.

"I'm fine," she waved her hand in the air and walked in the office. "Shut the door," she ordered.

After the door was shut, she pulled on the handle to make sure. She turned around and pulled the glasses off her face. Her outside appearance might seem as though she were put together but her eyes, her tunnel to her soul, told me differently. Her eyelids were bright red and the caked on makeup under her eyes tried to hide the black patches above her cheeks.

"I'm so not fine," she sobbed, dropping down on the couch.

"I'm so sorry." I gulped, rushing over to her to try to comfort her.

A jolt of electricity ran through me when I put my hands on her.

"What?" She looked up at me, sadness on her face.

"Nothing." My lips formed a thin line, the smile didn't reach my eyes. I sucked in a deep breath and put my hands around her in a sweet embrace and tried to get my intuition to tell me what the jolt was about.

"Burt really wasn't a bad guy." For some reason she wanted to tell me their story.

I really did try to listen, but there was an overwhelming sense in my gut that she wasn't truly sad, but not sure how to express her real feelings.

"Burt was so smart and funny." She painted a picture of a perfect man. "He was older and wise. I met him at the bar on the edge of town, Mac's, and we clicked. He asked me what I did, I told him. He was in between jobs so I offered him a job on the assembly line." She dabbed her eyes with the edge of the sleeve of her shirt. I got up and went to the bathroom to get her a tissue as she kept talking. "He came to my office and told me a more effective way to make the production line more efficient. I tried it and it worked. Head To Toe Works wouldn't be what it is today without him and he knew it." Her chin lifted. It trembled. "That is when he started to become abusive. He knew he had me where he needed me. I learned to live with his stress, but his mother." Hatred dripped from her mouth. "She thought she could just take right on over."

"Your marriage?" I questioned to clarify.

"No. The business." She shook her head. "Burt made her head of marketing without telling me. We fought over it. She and Burt were going to take me to court over how much percentage they got in the company since they were pretty much running everything."

"What about your lawyer? Didn't you have him look at it?" I asked.

"Her." She rolled her eyes. "She isn't any help. She said that I'm a little too late by giving them so much responsibility because Burt and Jenny went through most of the money."

"And that is what you meant by my product might save the company?" I asked.

"I know your stress product will put us back in the black." She closed her eyes and took a deep breath. "I'm sad from the memories of how good Burt and I had it when we got married."

"How long have you been married?" I asked.

"Five years. First marriage for both." She shrugged. "I know we are old and my company was doing fine, not quite as big when we got married, but I loved his ideas and they worked until they spent all the money. And don't get me wrong, I'm very upset he is dead because I thought he would change after we got back in the black and we could make things better."

"I'm sure it's hard." I patted her hand and decided to ask her about the fight they had before he was killed. "Tell me about the fight the two of you had last night."

"What fight?" she asked and dabbed her eyes.

I grabbed her fingers and noticed she didn't have the fancy nails of the woman in Madame Torres's replay of the scene of the fight.

"Your nails," my voice drifted off in a hush whisper.

"I know they are ugly, but I'm allergic to most nail products and I bite them." She curled her fingers into a balled fist and placed them in her lap.

"You didn't have long nails last night?" I asked to make sure. "And you didn't have a fight after hours with Burt in front of the barbeque assembly line you are using for my product?" I had to be as specific as possible.

"No," she said. "I went to Mac's to have a stiff drink. How do you know Burt had a fight?"

"He had to have fought with someone." I could feel myself getting deeper and deeper into this investigation. Oscar told me to stay out of it, but it was proving hard for me to do that. "Did anyone see you at Mac's?"

"Mac." Her brows rose. "Do you think?" She lifted her hand to her mouth. "Am I a suspect? I mean, you were the one who was at the scene doing some sort of . . ." Her voice trailed off.

"Voodoo?" I nervously laughed. "I'm guessing the security guard told you that?"

"No, Pearl said everyone thinks you are some sort of weirdo like a witch or something."

"And you believe in witches?" I threw my head back and tried to give a good belly laugh, hoping she'd take the bait.

Mewl, mewl. Mr. Prince Charming did his own little nervous laugh and jumped up in my lap. I ran my fingers down his back. His back arched.

"Of course I don't, but there are people out there who like to believe they are and if that's the case, I don't need that publicity along with Burt's death." She had some underlying meaning to her words and it struck my soul.

"Are you saying that you might break our contract? Because I'm not a witch or anything of the sort. I'm just a homeopathic lotion maker who makes people feel better with natural herbs." I had to convince her to let me stay. The village was counting on me to bring in the extra income I had promised to give them. Plus I couldn't live with myself if I failed. "Plus, you need me in more ways than one."

"How so?" she questioned.

"First off with my product. You and I both know you are going to make money and it will bring you back in the black." The next reason had to be enough convincing for her to keep me. "I have a sneaky feeling I can help you figure out who killed Burt and why they want the police to think it's you."

"They really do think it's me?" She sobbed, bringing her hands to her face.

"The spouse is always the first suspect." I knew Oscar and the Elders told me not to say anything unless Mac was present, but I knew in my gut Tiffany didn't have anything to do with Burt's murder.

Someone wanted the police to believe it was her and get her out of the way and there was only one person I could think of that would benefit.

Jenny Rossen. Burt's mom.

First I needed to get my hands on Tiffany's contract where she gave Burt and his mom some of the company. If Burt had a will, did he give his shares to his mom or back to Tiffany?

"Did Burt have a will?" I asked.

"Yes." She nodded. "But I'm sure it has me listed as the beneficiary."

"I wouldn't be so sure." Like an alarm, my intuition kicked in, telling me Tiffany was going to be sorely disappointed.

CHAPTER THIRTEEN

"Good work." Mary Ellen appeared out of thin air. Her long black hair was pulled up into a bun on top of her head in a very elegant way. She had on a black body suit. She was long and lanky like a lean cat. She walked around my office with an aqua colored potion bottle in her hand. She pulled the wand out of the bottle and flung the liquid around the room, making sure to get all the corners saturated.

I didn't have to ask her what she was doing because in my gut I could sense it was an all-knowing potion. She was giving a jolt to my already alert senses.

"Nice way to stay in the business with the lotions because it's up to you to keep our heritage a secret." Walking slowly, her hips swayed. She turned on her heels and strode over to the desk. She picked up Madame Torres. "How are you today?"

"I'm divine, Mary." Madame Torres appeared. A big smile on her face. "I'm so glad to have you here keeping this one in line."

"Are you joking me?" I rolled my eyes and plucked Madame Torres out of Mary Ellen's grip. "You have been about zero help."

"I showed you the killer." Her face set in a vicious expression. "It's up to you to figure it out."

"Is this true?" The look on Mary Ellen's face mingled eagerness and tenderness. "If this is true, you need to tell me. I'm the one who was assigned this case and I have a concert in Dubai I would like to attend tomorrow night. I'm in fear I am going to have to cancel because of the mess you have gotten yourself into."

"She didn't show me the killer's face, but I have a sneaky suspicion who it might be and I'm going to follow up on my hunch." My eyes clouded with visions from Madame Torres's scene of the fight between Burt and the other woman. "Don't cancel your plans just yet. I need a little time."

"Time I can give you." She waved her hand in the air and disappeared as fast as she came. But not giving me the time she said she could, because Mac McGurtle was knocking on the door and let himself in, Tiffany Rossen following closely behind.

"June." He nodded, plopping his briefcase down on the desk. He scooted Madame Torres across the desk. "Madame Torres, Mr. Prince Charming." He greeted each one of my familiars as though it was no big deal that Tiffany was in the room.

His blue eyes looked at Tiffany. He broke into a leisurely smile and pushed his large black-rimmed glasses up on his fat nose before his thick fingers opened the briefcase.

"Shall we?" He put his hand out gesturing me to sit. "Now, we have an agreement here between two parties. Ms. Heal, my client, and Head To Toe Works, your company." He pulled the contract out and flipped a few pages and stuck it out for Tiffany to get a look. "My client is in no way held responsible for the couple of hundred bottles that went out into your stores today. It specifically states her homeopathic cures will be bottled in the bottles provided by my client, June Heal, and no other packaging material shall be used."

"Mac," I interrupted.

"June, Order of the Elders." He jabbed the paper with his thick finger and continued to give Tiffany the business. "Therefore, you have no legal right to put those bottles on the shelf with my client's name on them. Any questions?" He looked up over the rims of his glasses.

"Mac," I nodded my head. "Can I see you in the bathroom for a second?"

Without a word between us, I gave the one-second finger gesture to Tiffany and shut the bathroom door behind Mac and myself.

"I have taken care of it." I gave him a quick run down of what I had done with the bottles and gave them the okay to ship them, but in the process happened upon the dead body of Burt. "I think that is why the Marys called you in. For some strange reason the security guard thinks I killed Burt."

"I see." Mac rubbed his chin and looked into the air. "I told the Elders this was not a good idea for you to take your potions out of the Village. I told them that after we got you in Whispering Falls to keep you there and now look. I must go see Oscar."

In a flash he was gone.

"Great!" I threw my hands in the air. "How am I going to explain to Tiffany where you went?" Keeping up with the lies I was having to tell to keep my heritage a secret was getting hard to keep up with.

"Tiffany," I planted a fake grin on my face and shut the bathroom door behind me. "Do you mind giving me and Mac a few minutes alone? I'll have this all straightened up in a few minutes."

"Okay." There was hesitation in her voice. "Do you think you could come down and look at the bottles when you get a second? And we do have that meeting with the board about your product."

"I thought in light of what happened with Burt that it was going to be cancelled?" It seemed very strange to continue business as usual when a major player in the Head To Toe Works company was murdered.

"It's still a business," she stated. "Did Apple shut down when Steve Jobs died?"

She had a good point. Only Head To Toe Works was not Apple.

I gave her a few minutes to get on with whatever she was doing before I decided to go to the factory and check out my products on the new line with the real bottles.

I was happy to see that Pearl was on the front of the line of Gentle

June's. She seemed to be the one who really championed the bottle and stood up for me when Josh was betting I was a witch.

"How is everything going?" I asked and noticed how nice the bottles looked. The pale yellow bottles were in the shape of a genie bottle. The lid was a pump so they didn't have any type of caps to pull off and the customer didn't have to unscrew it to get the little leftover on the bottom out.

"Just fine." Pearl looked me up and down. "Are you sure you ain't no witch or do some sort of voodoo shit?"

"Why would you say something like that?" I asked. "Do I look like a witch?"

"No, but that video the security guard put on YouTube sure does look like it." Josh's brow rose an inch.

"He did what?" I shuddered inwardly at the thought of something like this getting out. It was exactly what the Marys were afraid of.

But no, I had to practically beg them to let me do this when they had their meeting with the Village Council members.

"Yep." Pearl nodded her head, but didn't skip a beat putting the bottles in the machine to get filled up with my stress free lotions. "Search 'Burt Rossen's killer'."

"Ouch." I shook my wrist when it felt hot and looked down. The liquid in the potion bottle charm was bubbling. "Is that guard here this morning?"

"He is." Josh pointed to the offices up above. "He had a meeting with some policeman about the discovery. He swears you were doing some voodoo chant. Said he was going to call the news too."

"Not if I can help it." I bolted out of the factory and up the steps.

Harm to none; that was what Bella had told me about the liquid inside the potion charm. But what did that mean?

"I'm going to have to cancel the meeting today." I informed Tiffany after I had gone to the security station looking for that guard. He was nowhere to be found. "I have an emergency in Whispering Falls."

Tiffany looked up at me from her desk. Her makeup ran down her face.

"Maybe you should go home." I suggested when I noticed all the pictures of her and Burt scattered all over the top of her desk. "Even if you and Burt didn't have the best relationship, you were still married, you shared a life together."

"I loved him," she sputtered through sobs. "And I'm afraid he never loved me. It was all a sham."

"What are you talking about?" I didn't understand what she was telling me.

"We are done for." She shook her head and picked up a piece of paper off the desk. "After you asked me about the will, I called our lawyer. Burt and Jenny had recently redone his will to make her his executrix and leave her all his shares of the company if something were to happen to him. It not only gives her two-thirds of the company once the estate settles, but immediate control right away between her shares and her power over Burt's shares in his estate."

"That doesn't mean Head To Toe Works is finished." The more I thought about this Jenny woman; the more and more she began to become a suspect. What mother would kill her son? A greedy one.

"I just got off the phone with her. She's ordered the production line to be shut down as of right now." Tiffany hung her head. "I'm sorry, June. It's over. There is no amount of Gentle June that will take this much stress away."

It was hard trying to swallow the big pill of failure. Not accomplishing what I had set out to do didn't sit well with my soul, or maybe it was my intuition nagging me. The fight between Burt and the woman the night of his death could be the link Oscar needed to help find the killer.

It wasn't like I felt the woman killed Burt. There were plenty of women who worked in the factory, but only one I had seen him grab. Tiffany. This woman was the second. The logical situation was the woman killed him and put him on the conveyor belt, only Burt wasn't the smallest of men. And I couldn't help but think the woman in the fight Madame Torres showed me would be capable of hoisting Burt on the conveyor belt.

The ride to the Locust Grove Police Station seemed much longer than usual. The feeling of guilt for my village who had put so much confidence in me going outside of our community to bring extra income to the village weighed heavy on me. Telling Oscar the deal had not even come to fruition made it real. More real than I was ready to deal with.

Plus I had brought the Marys and Mac McGurtle into the mix with all the contracts and to make sure no one outside of our village found out who the resident of Whispering Falls really was.

"Here goes nothing," I murmured under my breath when I put the Green Machine in park.

The lights in the parking lot led my way into the station. It was getting dark and I knew I might have been cutting it close to when Oscar was off his shift.

"June, how are you?" Sonny asked when I walked in.

He had strawberry-blond hair with freckles dotted around his face. His jaw was square and he had a nice deep smile. He wasn't the handsomest of men, but he sure was reliable and good-hearted from what my intuition told me.

"Hi, Sonny." I gave a slight wave and glanced around the room looking for Oscar. "Is Oscar around?"

"I let him get home. He worked late on the Head To Toe Works homicide last night. Which reminds me," he stood up and tugged on the belt, pulling his pants up around his gut. "Oscar said you had been working there or something."

"Yes," I spoke loud and clear wondering if I should tell him about Jenny shutting down the facility and the will. Or maybe he already knew. "They purchased my stress free lotion I used to make for the Locust Grove Flea Market."

I had to choose my words wisely when around people who weren't familiar with me or Darla.

"I heard from around town how much they miss your mom, Darla is it?" he questioned.

"Darla," I confirmed.

"They miss your mom's booth at the market. But Oscar tells them about your shop in Whispering Falls." His eyes searched mine. I could tell he was trying to use his cop instinct to get a feel for me. I stood there, holding my own. "Quaint town."

"Oscar and I love it." I grinned from ear-to-ear.

"Congratulations by the way. I hear you haven't set a real date yet." Sonny was digging. Was he digging for the investigation or for Oscar?

"Soon. Anyway, how is the investigation going?" I asked. "Any suspects?"

"Too early. What do you know about Tiffany?" he asked.

"On the record or off?" I had listened to Oscar so many times that I sort of knew when to talk and when not to.

"We are just talking here, June." He settled back in his chair with his hands folded over his chest. "Anything you can tell me to bring a killer to justice would be nice."

"I don't know a whole lot. They had come to Whispering Falls over Christmas and Burt seemed to cater to her. He was the one who really wanted my product in the stores initially." My voice lowered.

"Initially?" His ears perked and he sat up, this time with his hand clasped and resting on the desk in front of him.

"In Whispering Falls, but when it came time to bottling the product, I found they weren't using the bottles I had given them at no cost and were instead using cheap plastic ones." I shrugged. "I thought we had gotten the issue resolved."

"That was why you were there last night? Because it seems to me if you thought the issue was resolved, you wouldn't have to go back after hours." His tone put caution in the air between us.

"Are you accusing me of doing something?" I asked to make clear I was understanding him.

"Just answer the question." He shrugged, his eyes narrowed.

"I have nothing to hide." Though I did know the Elders didn't want me to say anything to anyone without Mac present. "I went there to make sure the bottles were going to be ready for the assembly line the next morning for work. We were already a day behind and as you know, time is money. That's how any company works."

"You have been taken off the suspect list." He picked up the pen off his desk and tapped it on the file that read ROSSEN.

"Glad to know, but I didn't realize I was a suspect." That was a lie. I knew enough to know that everyone was a suspect until it was whittled down.

"The security camera showed you trying to get in through the security gate and Mr. Rossen was shot hours before you got there." His chest heaved up and then down when he took a big deep breath before letting it out in a slow steady stream. "And his wife was in the hospital when I went to question her for a case of the nerves."

"Really?" I bit back the desire to tell him that I had just come from the headquarters and she was fine and dandy. "And I'm trying to locate his mother, Jenny Rossen, but she hasn't turned up."

"She hasn't?" I gasped, knowing the will between mother and son was a good reason to kill and how Jenny could now have a majority of the company.

"Nope." He shook his head. "It's like she doesn't exist. But I'm not done looking. I heard a lot of those workers go to Mac's, that bar on the other side of town, after supper. I think they know something they aren't telling me."

His words struck my gut. Doesn't exist? Jenny does. At least that was why and how I had met Tiffany in the first place. The dreaded stress of the mother-in-law. Plus Pearl or Josh knew something. At least Faith said one of them, he or Pearl, and he seemed to be the likely one since he seemed to have his ear in everyone's conversations. It was about time I stepped my witchy toes inside of Mac's.

CHAPTER FOURTEEN

"They what?" Raven Mortimer poured a cup of hot coffee from the freshly brewed pot and set it between us. She merely stared, tongue-tied. Her black hair was pulled back in a clip and she wore a pink apron with the Wicked Good Bakery Logo written in lime green.

Wicked Good Bakery was closed when I finally made it back to Whispering Falls, but it didn't stop me from knocking on the door when I saw Raven working on the next day's pastries. I needed a little June's Gem fix to kill the stress of talking to Sonny about the case. I'd kept my little secret about Burt's change in his will to myself. I really wanted to tell Oscar and let him do with it what he needed to do.

"Jenny, the new CEO and Burt's mom, halted production. Everything. The entire product line." I picked up the delicate china cup and took a sip. I picked up the June's Gem and sunk my teeth into it. I closed my eyes and let the chocolaty goodness settle the nerve war going on inside of me. "Not only that, but Burt changed his will for his mom to get his portion of the business which. . ."

"Automatically gives her more shares and control of the business." Raven's jaw dropped, she held the tiny cup in front of her face. "Why would she halt production? If she's the new CEO wouldn't she want to make the business last?"

"Good question." My mind began to turn a million miles a minute trying to come up with every excuse in the book on why Jenny would want the company to die. "Burt seemed happy about the lotion idea at Christmas, but when I was there yesterday for my first day, he tried to pull a fast one on me and use cheap plastic bottles."

I took the time to explain to Raven exactly why my bottles were important and why I had gone there last night to put a little magical touch on them.

"I just couldn't let them go out like that in good faith." There was one thing I had to do. Go see Jenny Rossen. "Thanks for the coffee. I have to go."

"You aren't going to do something stupid are you?" There was doubt in her question because she knew I was going to do something that Oscar would not approve of.

"You don't want to know," I assured her and took another sip of my coffee.

"I don't want to add to your stress, but I had a couple of visitors today." Raven gazed at me with a half smile. "Helena and Eloise."

"Ugh!" My jaw clamped tight and I could feel the tension creeping up in my veins.

"They wanted to make sure I was available during our All Hallows Eve festivities for a catering job for a wedding." Her smile went wry.

"I guess I don't have to tell you how much this displeases me." I tapped the edge of the cup thinking how I just didn't need this right now.

"They want me to make cupcakes with your initials on them. I couldn't help but watch as they left." She bit the corner of her lip as though she were trying to keep her mouth shut.

"Go on. You can't stop now." At this point I feared there was no stopping the two aunts.

"They went into The Gathering Grove. They were in there for a while." Raven got up and walked behind the counter. She grabbed a couple of June's Gems, put them on a plate and brought them back, setting them between us. She sat down and took one of the chocolaty tasty treats and sunk her teeth into it. I followed suit. She mumbled with a mouthful, "Gerald came over to get the last of his muffin order and I asked him about it."

"And?" I encouraged her.

"They paid him in full to do the catering for a wedding reception on All Hallows Eve." The pain in her eyes matched the pain in my heart.

"Did you know that Oscar and I were an arranged marriage from the get go?" I knew she didn't know, but it was how it came out.

"No way!" Her eyes practically popped out of her head.

"We didn't know this when we fell in love." Then it hit me. "O-M-G," I gasped. "Do you think they put a spell on us to fall in love?"

"No." Raven brushed it off, but I could tell she was thinking about it, not fully convinced of her answer. "Do you?"

"We grew up across the street from each other so the village could keep an eye on us and we didn't fall in love until we moved to Whispering Falls after we found out we were spiritualists." An uneasy feeling churned deep inside of me. "When I found out I was a Good-Sider, I fainted. When I came to, everyone was around me, including Oscar. They had told him about our heritage while I was out. I clearly remember Izzy giving me something to drink." I dug in my memory to try to recall what it was.

"By law a spiritualist cannot do magic on another." Raven made a good point.

"But," I snapped my fingers, "if I didn't know I was a spiritualist at the time, then the law didn't pertain to me. And." Memories of the day Oscar and I found out about who we really were flooded my mind. "We also went to The Gathering Grove where I clearly remember Gerald giving us tea."

"Oh June." Raven stood up and picked up our cups. She spoke with her back to me and put the dishes away behind the counter. "Oscar loves you and you love him. I can see it in his eyes."

"But is it real? Or is it a spell?" I questioned the validity of what I'd thought was authentic love between us. "I wouldn't put it past the two aunts to make sure we were destined to be together."

"They seemed pretty sure you were going to tie the knot on All Hallows Eve." Raven shrugged and plopped a big ball of dough on top of the stainless steel counter. She fisted her hands and plunged them in the dough, kneading it, throwing flour on it, and kneading it some more. She flipped it, patted it and rolled it into a ball before she started the process all over again.

"This is just one more thing to add to my growing list." There was no time to waste. I had to go to the shop and make sure everything was ready for tomorrow and customers. Even though my business outside of Whispering Falls seemed to be crumbling, I still had to focus on A Charming Cure. "Tell Faith thanks for taking care of the shop today."

"She loves it." Raven waved me off as I went out the door.

The moon was so full and shone over top of Whispering Falls like a spot light. All the shops were closed and the carriage lights glowed. A few of the teenagers, disguised as fireflies, darted in and out of the nighttime shadows as if they were playing catch. When I first came to live at Whispering Falls, I had gotten myself into a little pickle and the fireflies really helped me out by letting Petunia know something was wrong. At the time I had no idea people who had passed on sometimes came back as animals and very surprised to find out fireflies were teenagers whose lives had been cut short way too early.

It did make sense. Most teens I knew stayed up late and slept most of the day, so being a firefly was probably a good animal for them to come back as.

I looked at Mr. Prince Charming darting across the street in front of me. My eyes narrowed. Could he be? Was he alive as human before? It was a question I had never asked. I took him for what I was told he was. My fairy-god cat.

I opened the gate, ran my fingers along the wisteria vine around the trellis, getting a big sense of my mother. I shook it off because there was no time to get sentimental. I had to figure out why my product line was axed before I got a visit from Mary Ellen.

Meow. Mr. Prince Charming danced at the door wanting in.

"You aren't someone I know, are you?" I asked him while jabbing my key in the door. I laughed to myself when he started to lick himself. "I guess that's my answer."

The inside of the shop was dark and I flipped on the light.

"Oh my God!" My lips thinned with anger. My nostrils flared with fury as I looked around and noticed every single table had been over-turned and every bottle had been broken, smashed into pieces.

"June! What happened?" Constance Karima, owner of Two Sisters and A Funeral, appeared at the door. Patience Karima, her sister, stood behind her. Both grey-haired women scurried inside to get a good look.

"What happened?" Patience, who had a habit of repeating her sister, stood behind Constance attached to her pet ostrich.

The sisters looked up at me with wonder in their sparkly green eyes.

The ostrich pecked away at the remaining liquid and lotions on the floor.

"Move that bird!" I screamed and pointed to the door. "Run over and get Oscar or Colton!"

Patience attempted to climb on the back of her bird. After a couple of times trying to get her leg lifted, Constance stomped over.

"Here." Constance grounded herself like a tree and interlocked her fingers together, giving Patience a foot saddle to help her up. Only Patience laid belly first on the bird and Constance swatted its feathery butt. Patience screamed the entire way down the road and across the street with her legs dangling behind her.

"Oh, June. Someone is after you." The tone in Constance's voice made me flinch. "Maybe you'll be my next customer."

"Don't count on it," I grumbled under my breath.

CHAPTER FIFTEEN

"And you didn't see anyone or anything funny?" Oscar asked Raven, Chandra and Arabella as they stood in a circle inside A Charming Cure.

They were the only shop owners still in their shops after closing. They all shook their heads.

"I was so busy creating and bringing wilted flowers back to life that I wasn't paying attention to anything but the colorful world of my own." Arabella glanced around the room. "June, I will help replace all the special ingredients you can get from my flowers and special petals." Her generosity spread.

"And I'll pluck some drowsy daisy to get you started." Chandra knew the magical flower loved so much by Darla was in most of Darla's homeopathic cures in the Magical Cures Book where she journaled and left so many secret potions in there for me.

"That is so nice of you, Chandra." Oscar put his police notebook back in his pocket. He rubbed his hand down my back. "I'm sure June appreciates it."

"Oh," his touch brought me out of my thoughts, "yes, I do appreciate any help."

I rushed behind the counter where I kept the Magical Cures Book.

"June?" Oscar hurried behind me.

"The book." I couldn't help but feel like someone wanted something. I moved the extra cauldron from underneath the counter and the book was safely tucked away. I held it close to my chest and rocked back and forth. "Whoever broke in here doesn't know about the book. They wanted something else and when they didn't find it," my voice trailed off.

"What?" Oscar asked. "June?"

"It has to be related to Head To Toe Works. Someone really doesn't want my lotion to hit the shelves of the store." I bit the edge of my lip, trying to think about what they could possibly want.

I glanced around the shop.

"Think about it." I pointed to the shelf of empty potion bottles behind me. "The bottles weren't broken because there wasn't anything in there. All the ingredient bottles and bottles that contained something have been busted."

"I think you are right." Raven's eyes drew down. "Tonight, after you left, a picture of a graveyard continued to pop up in the dough. I never even thought it could be about what was going on in Locust Grove with the murder of Burt because it wasn't here in Whispering Falls. Plus I was figuring it wasn't about you. I thought if I was going to have a vision in the dough about you, it was going to be about the wedding or All Hallows Eve."

"Our wedding?" Oscar's face contorted. "All Hallows Eve?"

"Long story." I touched his arm. "I'll tell you later." I turned back to Raven. "Anything other than a graveyard?" I curled my hands back around the book and held it tight.

Raven's eyes dropped down and focused on the book. She gulped. She licked her lips and looked up at me with concern.

"That book." Her finger lifted and pointed to the Magical Cures Book. "It was in my dough."

We all stood in silence. They didn't know what it meant but I did. I had to go to my mother's grave. There had to be something with the graveyard and the book. I was going to have to pay a visit to my mom.

"We can get this all cleaned up in no time." I wasn't sure when I would make the time to see Darla, I just knew the shop took priority.

"June, we need to get fingerprints and go over the crime scene." Oscar tried to stop me from flipping the switch on my cauldron. "You can close one day to get things in order. You don't have to do this tonight."

"Yes I do!" The anger flew out of me. "You don't understand! This is what I have worked for all of my life! This!" I twirled around the room. "This is my life. It's all I know. You are my life. Or at least I thought you were until I found out that we are arranged by our families to be married."

"We are what?" He froze into blankness.

"June," Raven called my name, but it didn't stop me.

"Yeah. Do we really love each other? Or are we merely a spell for our families to carry on our heritage?" Tears stung my eyes. I blinked. The salt water dripped down my cheeks.

"I think you are a little stressed." Chandra picked up the broom. "I'll sweep up and you can go rest."

"I'm fine," I said flatly. There was a hurt look in Oscar's eyes. He looked as though he were trying to wrap his head around what I was suggesting.

"Spell or not, I love you." Oscar watched as I touched the different bottles behind me.

"Eye of newt, pond spleen, moonstone, star thistle." As I said the name and touched the bottle, it filled with the ingredient. "Snake oil, witch's wart, bat wing, fingernails, toenails, lacewing, wolf's bane, stardust, tiger whiskers."

And the list went on. Within a few minutes, I had restocked my ingredient shelf except for one. The wisteria vine oil. It was not extracted from a witch's hand but a mortal hand. According to the Magical Cures Book, Darla had spent a better part of her time in Whispering Falls extracting the potent oil for the village to use. It was the main ingredient in my stress free lotion.

"Wisteria vine oil." The words almost burnt my lips as they rolled off my tongue.

"What?" Oscar asked. The hurt of my words had deepened.

"They came in and stole the wisteria vine oil. It had to be someone at the factory who really didn't want me to make any more stress free lotion for Head To Toe Works."

"Are you sure?" Oscar looked around at the broken bottles behind the counter.

"I'm positive. Somehow they figured out the ingredient and since it's so hard to extract from the vine, they knew I was the maker and came in here to steal what I had." It was a definite reason to break into my shop. "Everyone," I hollered throughout the shop to get their attention. "I want to thank you for coming to my side tonight to help me, but I think I'm going to call it a night and do what Oscar asks. Shut down tomorrow and try to get some new homeopathic base cures together so I can open in a couple of days."

"You let me know if you need any more drowsy daisy." Chandra patted my back. "I have plenty."

"And I'll keep you in June's Gems to help out with the stress. Faith is also available after her morning pastry drop off at the Piggly Wiggly." Raven wiggled her fingers at us before she left.

"I have plenty of leftover floral herbs and seeds I will gather and bring to you in the morning." Arabella reached out and squeezed my hand. "Remember, Oscar adores you no matter what."

I thanked them all from the front steps of A Charming Cure and waved them off into the dark night.

CHAPTER SIXTEEN

"Now we can get down to business." I locked the door and pulled the shop shades down real tight so no moonlight or even the smallest firefly could see in.

"Somehow the murder and the break-in have to be tied." Oscar got his notebook out and made a diagram on a piece of paper with Burt's name at the top. "Who are the people you have met so far?"

"Obviously there is Tiffany." I watched as Oscar wrote down her name. "But I honestly don't think it was her."

"It's usually the spouse and that is who Sonny is looking at very closely." Oscar's brow lifted as he talked about the murder investigation Locust Grove Sheriff Sonny Butcher was conducting.

There was something so sexy when he flicked on his internal cop guy attitude. Surely those feelings weren't created by a spell.

"Madame Torres showed me something was happening in the factory before I had even gone there that night. It was a fight between Burt and someone dressed almost exactly like Tiffany. I had Madame Torres play the scene over and over." I grabbed my bag off the chair behind the counter where I had put it when I came in and I dug Madame Torres out of the bottom.

"Madame Torres, please show me the video of Burt and the woman arguing." I tapped the coal black globe.

"You have got to be kidding me," sarcasm dripped from deep within the globe. Her face appeared with a white film over it. Her lips were still blood red. "How do you expect me to perform at my best if you insist on keeping me up at all hours of the night?" She yawned.

"Garage sale." It was the magical two words to keep her quiet and do what I had asked.

Oscar bent down and watched as the scene of Burt grasping the bottle and fighting with the woman played out.

"See there," I pointed to the woman's hand, "she had nails and Tiffany is allergic to nail polish."

"She told you this?" he asked.

"Yes." I nodded. "I did see Burt grab her by the face in a forceful way the other day and she apologized to me saying how he worked for her in the factory before they were married. They met at Mac's one night and Burt was out of work. That's when she hired him. Once he started working there he continued to come to her with more efficient ways to run the company. Recently they were having some financial difficulty. They asked his mother, Jenny Rossen, for some financial assistance. This was all during their Christmas visit."

I stopped until I saw Oscar was caught up on writing everything I was saying down.

"Go on," he encouraged me.

"Tiffany gave Burt twenty-six percent of the company and Jenny twenty-five percent of the company leaving her with forty-nine percent for majority. Over the past few weeks, Burt had changed his will making his mother the beneficiary of his holdings, giving her the majority in the company, making her CEO."

"And if she and Tiffany didn't get along like at Christmas time, she would have reason to want to not move forward with Gentle June's if she could get her hands on the lotion's ingredients." Oscar was using his sleuthing skills and looked ever so handsome doing it.

"That is something I hadn't thought of." My intuition told me he was on to something. "But the joke is really on them because the magic is really in the bottle."

"Of course they don't know that." Oscar's lips turned up. His eyes sparkled, sending tingly chills all over my body. "But who killed Burt?"

"I don't know." I closed my eyes and thought long and hard about what my next step needed to be. "Maybe the two aren't tied. After Burt was killed and Jenny knew my product was going to save the line, she came here and broke in, destroying everything. Only I'm not sure how she would know that wisteria vine oil was in the lotion. If she could squeeze Tiffany out and make the product herself, she sees it as a win/win."

Josh and Pearl popped into my head.

"There is Josh, the tattoo guy." I pointed to Oscar's notepad for him to write down Josh's name and stirred the bubbling cauldron. "He and Burt had words about the packaging of my lotion when I noticed they were using those cheap bottles."

"Really?" Oscar wrote on the pad under Josh's name.

"Yeah. He said how packaging appealed to the customer." I stirred the cauldron one more time before I put the ladle down and walked around the counter toward the door. Somehow I was going to have to get that wisteria vine oil. "I think he's right. Did you see those cheap bottles?" I asked and opened the door.

Whispering Falls was so pretty at night. The stars dotted the sky, looking like twinkling lights. They shone down with the moon into the valley of the village, putting a silent glow around the town. It added to the magical community.

A sense of safety crept into my soul. I sucked in a deep breath of the fresh nighttime air. I felt safe, believing the person who broke into the shop was definitely not from Whispering Falls.

I reached out and grabbed a piece of the wisteria vine. I had seen Darla countless times run her fingers down the shoot, knocking the flowering off of it. After that I wasn't sure what she did. Most of the time she shoo'ed me out of the shed so she could do her creating.

"That doesn't really give Josh a reason to kill Burt." Oscar said to me when I walked back in the shop and he tapped his little notebook with the tip of his pen.

"Burt embarrassed him after that asking if Josh was now the marketing manager." I twirled the broken vine in the air trying to figure out exactly how I was to extract the oil.

I walked back around the counter to the cauldron, looked at the vine one more time and tugged my fingers down the shoot, knocking off all the flowering pieces. I threw the vine in the pot hoping something would come to me.

"And Pearl." I picked up the ladle and blended the vine into the bubbling cauldron. "She and Burt had words because she told him how and where to package my lotion using my bottles."

"Well, since you are not a suspect and Sonny is in charge, I think we just give him this information and let him figure it out." He walked behind the counter and looked in the pot. "Do me a favor and let's just cut ties with Head To Toe Works."

The mixture in my pot boiled and suddenly stopped, becoming chunky in an ochre color.

"Nasty." Irritated, I flipped off the cauldron. "You know," I threw the ladle on the counter, "there is no magic to what Darla did to the stem. Why can't I do it?"

"You don't need to do it." Oscar's voice was a little huskier. "We will tell Sonny about the break-in and when it's solved, if it's tied to Burt's murder, we will figure it out. In the meantime, we will add more security to the shop and life will go back to the way it was before you met the Rossens."

I grabbed the Magical Cures Book and flipped it open, turning the pages until I came to the page with the recipe I had used for the stress free lotion. If I didn't say a word to Oscar, I wouldn't lie to him because I knew I couldn't let this go. There was evil in the air and it was up to me to figure out who had gotten their hands on my cure.

"June," Oscar set the pen on the counter next to his notebook. "Can we talk for a minute?"

"About us?" My heart skipped a beat. I knew I wasn't going to be able to ignore the elephant in the room. "I had a dream about my dad."

"You did?" Oscar encircled me in his arms, one of his hands rested on the small of my back. "Why didn't you tell me?"

"I don't know." A happy sigh escaped me. There was no way I was under some sort of spell put on me by the village or the Elders or our parents. I loved Oscar. I had always loved Oscar.

He ran his hand down my cheek. The mere touch of his hand sent a warming shiver throughout my body.

"Tell me about it," he said with quiet emphasis.

"I thought it might be one of my dreams but I think it is just the stress of not having them here." I nuzzled in his neck. His natural smell was better than any cologne and there was no way it could be bottled. Gently my lips kissed his neck a few times. "I'm sure it's my subconscious playing with me because in my dream I was at the cemetery looking at their stones. My dad sat next to me."

I looked up. His blue eyes studied my face.

"Your parents would be so proud of you." Oscar's lips came down warm and sweet on mine. He whispered, "As for any sort of marriage arrangement, even if there were such a contract, I'm happy they got it right."

I smiled. He was right. If there were a contract, my parents and his parents knew we would be good together. They were right.

"And maybe you should go visit the cemetery. Talk to them like they are living." He swooped me up in his arms. I wrapped my arms around his neck and he took me to the storage room where I had a small living space, including a couch.

CHAPTER SEVENTEEN

I lay in the curve of Oscar's body, listening to him slightly snore. Being with him confirmed even more how much I couldn't wait to become Mrs. Oscar Park.

"June Park." I grinned at the sound of it as my married name came out of my mouth. "June Park."

I glanced out the storage room door and out into the shop. Regardless of what happened with Head To Toe Works, my life was good. But I still couldn't shake why someone would want my recipe.

"KJ," I gasped remembering just how I could get my hand on some wisteria vine oil.

Slowly I lifted Oscar's arm from around me and rested it on his own hip. He shifted a bit and I waited to get up until I heard him snoring again, leaving him in the storage room.

Rowl. Mr. Prince Charming lifted his head from the stool where he was curled up.

"You stay here." I grabbed my cloak off the coat rack and threw it over my shoulders. "I'll be right back."

I let myself out the front door and swept down the steps. I walked up to the hill behind the shop to The Gathering Rock. It was a space just before the wooded area where Eloise lived. There was a large rock where the villagers gathered during celebrations and meetings. I also used it to get in touch with KJ, the son of Kenny.

Kenny was a Native American that helped supply me with the special herbs only he could get me from his native land. Unfortunately, Kenny was killed, but his son KJ had taken over for him. KJ always knew when I needed smudging grass or my regular ingredients. The bottles told him when they were getting low. When I needed something special, like wisteria vine oil, I would message him through the wind.

The wind whipped around me. The fireflies batted around the rock, darting in and out of the woods. The rustle of the trees told me it was time.

I breathed into the wind as soon as it passed through me, sending a signal out into the universe for KJ. Out of the corner of my eye, the images of a graceful deer leapt out of the woods. Long and dark, KJ appeared on the edge of The Gathering Rock with his arms crossed over his bare chest and a feather headdress atop his long black hair.

"KJ, I'm so glad to see you." I rushed over and greeted him. "How is your family?"

"They are good." He reached around his back and pulled his knapsack to the front of him. He reached in and pulled out a black clay vase with two spouts. "From my family."

He held it out.

"It's a Native American wedding vase we made for you." As I held it in my hands, he pointed to the various parts. "The two drinking spouts are connected by a single handle. The two spouts symbolize the two individual lives, and the handle symbolizes the union of these two lives in marriage. You and Oscar."

"I love it, KJ!" I threw my arms around his neck, knowing he wouldn't reciprocate. When I pulled away, he had a faint smile on his lips. "It's our first wedding gift."

"I hope you enjoy." He nodded.

"I have two favors." I felt like a schoolgirl inside with my first request. "Oscar and I would be honored if you would marry us on All Hallows Eve here in The Gathering Rock space."

It was request I knew Oscar wouldn't mind if I handled on my own. We didn't have anyone to marry us and KJ was the perfect choice for our spiritualist wedding.

"I would be honored." He bowed, his headdress fanning me.

"I know I'm not Native American and neither is Oscar, but we would love to have the ceremony." I had been to a couple since I was a spiritualist and we loved them. It was two families coming together and there was not a more beautiful ceremony than a Native American marriage.

"You be sure you bring the vase." KJ's arms extended down to his side. "What else can I do for you?"

"I need to get my hands on some wisteria vine oil." I glanced down the hill toward the village. Everything was still asleep and quiet. "Darla was the only person I knew who had extracted oil from a vine and I just can't figure it out."

"You must take a vine to the graveyard and tell the maker what you seek for I do not have the vine nor the oil for you." KJ turned and darted off into the woods.

"Tell the maker?" I questioned into the wind.

"The maker," the wind called back.

"June," Oscar and Mr. Prince Charming were climbing the hill. "Are you okay?"

"I'm good. I just needed some fresh air." Though I knew Oscar didn't believe me, he didn't ask me anything else.

"I woke up and you weren't next to me." He drew me in from behind and wrapped his arms around me, resting his face on my shoulder. Both of us looking down the hill. "Isn't the village beautiful?"

"Yes. And the stars." I swallowed hard and bit back tears. There was something deep within me churning and I couldn't put my finger on it.

"Baby, what's wrong?" Oscar turned me around.

"I don't know why I'm so emotional." I swallowed hard. "I'm thinking it's getting married without any of our parents, plus the fact someone stole the last of Darla's vine oil. It was the only herb I had left that was part of her. And to think it was probably because of some silly national deal."

"Don't worry." He tucked a strand of my hair behind my ear and pulled my chin up to look at him. "Sonny will figure out who stole it if it's related to Burt Rossen's death and we will get it back."

"You are too good to me, Oscar Park." I placed my hand on the back of his neck and drew him down to me. His lips parted mine in a soul-reaching kiss. "I can't wait to say I do on All Hallows Eve."

"So is that the date?" he asked. I nodded. He threw back his head and let out a great peal of laughter. "I love you June Heal Park."

CHAPTER EIGHTEEN

Luckily with no dreams or nightmares, I was able to get some sleep, but I knew I had a full day of work ahead. Before Oscar and I headed home we had cleaned up the shop and refilled the potion bottles enough to open. I would make a few special cures while customers where milling around and have Faith watch the shop while I went to see my parents.

KJ's words were the first thing that popped into my head.

The cauldron was good and clean when I flipped it on. I ran my hand down the shelf of ingredients behind me. I grabbed the geranium, beeswax, rosewater, coconut oil and pinched or poured a few drops into the cauldron.

"Now." I brushed my hands above the cauldron. "I'll let you simmer."

The clock said it was time to flip the sign and get ready for the day.

"I'll be right with you," I called after I had turned the sign to open and gone back to the counter hiding behind the partition where my cauldron was coming to a boil. The glowing liquid was exactly what it was supposed to look like before I put in the wisteria vine oil. The sapphire color swirled counter-clockwise until it reached a state of ruby globules.

"June?" The voice called out from underneath the dinging bell above the door. "It's Pearl and Josh!"

"Pearl. Josh?" I stuck my head around the corner and saw them standing in the doorway of the shop. Both of them glancing around.

"What kind of store is this?" Pearl had a box in her hand.

"It's like a mini Head To Toe Works, only cuter stuff." Josh picked up a long thin glass bottle with wire wrapping coiled around it. Evenly spaced glass beads were held tight to the bottle by the wire. The cork lid had a little silver fairy sitting on top of it. "Sleep aid?" He read the label before putting it back down.

"Welcome." I wiped my hands down my apron and greeted them. "Why aren't you at work?"

"Tiffany came in and shut us down." Pearl put the box on the ground. "I took these and thought you might want them back."

"How did you know where to find me?" I asked and pointed to the small table near the front where I had some hot apple cider from The Gathering Grove simmering in a crock-pot for my customers.

"Tiffany put the bottles out at the dumpster." Josh picked up another bottle and read the label. "Seriously, why on earth would you want to sell your product through Head To Toe?"

"It was the national thing." I wasn't going to lie. "I care about my customers and if a large chain like Head To Toe Works can get my product in the hands of the American people, I was all for it."

Pearl wasn't as interested in the shop as Josh was. She just stood by the door with her hands clasped in front of her.

"We only came to drop off the bottles. There are more in the car." Pearl opened the door and walked out.

"Is she okay?" I asked Josh.

"No, dude. She's mad. We are both mad as hell." He popped off the lid of one of the sleeping aids and took a whiff. "But she's already got a new job taking care of some old lady."

"Are you having a hard time sleeping?" I asked, ignoring Pearl putting another box in the shop.

"Nah, just curious about all of this." Josh pointed to the boxes of bottles. "It didn't seem right to keep those by the dumpster."

"Thanks, Josh and Pearl." I wasn't really sure what to say. It was their only job and I felt bad for them. "Do either of you know who would want to kill Burt?" I just couldn't do what Oscar asked me to do. I had to get to the bottom of it.

"Nope. He was a jerk, but he was the boss and I needed my job." Josh shrugged and looked over at Pearl.

"Don't look at me," Pearl quipped. "I kept my head down and did my job. I've got mouths to feed."

"You did get in a little tiff with him the other day." I recalled her talking about the different conveyor belt with the bottles I had provided.

"Yeah, but that doesn't give me reason to kill the man." Her eyes narrowed, creases formed between her eyes. "I don't think we are welcome here anymore."

"Pearl, I didn't mean to. . .," my voice lowered after they rushed out of the shop, "to insult you."

I stood out on the front stoop of A Charming Cure waving my arms trying to get them to stop so I could make a quick apology, but they just zoomed down the streets toward Locust Grove.

"Who was that?" Faith asked. She was walking up the street with two cups of coffee in her hand.

"No one," I said. "Please tell me one of those is for me."

"It is." She walked up the steps and handed me one. Our fingers grazed. Her head tilted. Her eyes went blank and in a stare that led over my shoulder. "One of them knows about the break-in."

"What?" I asked.

"One of those people who were just here knows something about the shop break-in." Her head turned in the direction of Josh and Pearl speeding out of town. She shook her head, her blond hair fell behind her shoulder. "Something told me you needed me today."

"Tell me what you know about the two who were just here." There was no way I was going to let her get away with just saying they knew about it. "Did they break in? What do you mean they know about it?"

"The voices whisper." Her eyes darted around the open morning air. "There are rumblings. Nothing real specific yet. Only they know something and they came here to tell you or give you clues for you to put together."

"They didn't say much." I opened the door. Mr. Prince Charming darted out and headed toward Glorybee. He loved going there in the morning when Petunia was feeding the animals. He loved to sit in the live tree in the store and visit with his animal friends. I held the door open for Faith.

"Did they mention your shop?" she asked.

"Pearl didn't say much. She brought me my bottles back. Josh said she found them by the dumpster." I shut the door behind us and walked back to the cauldron.

The only thing that really stuck with me was when Josh said he didn't understand why I would give Head To Toe Works my lotion when I had a shop here. Of course I told him to help customers, but I really wanted to do my share to help the economy in Whispering Falls since it was our few shops that kept us going.

"Congratulations by the way." Faith and I shared a smile.

I knew she was talking about me finally setting a wedding date.

"The air told me." She waved her hand in the air.

Hear ye, hear ye! The bells will be ringing on All Hallows Eve. Wedding bells, that is for our very own June Heal and Sheriff Oscar Park. KJ will be performing the marriage ceremony using a traditional Native American celebration complete with the wedding vase he and his family made for the Parks as a wedding gift. This means All Hallows Eve will be a big celebration full of spiritual happenings and fun. We will still host our annual open house, so start planning your shop's festival activities today! It will be here before you know it. This article is sponsored by Mystic Lights. Be sure to see Isadora Solstice for all your magic ball tune-ups and needs.

In other news, be sure to lock your doors. Sheriff Lance and Sheriff Park are still on the lookout for the person who ransacked and stole potions from A

Charming Cure. If your gift is telling you any details or if you saw something out of place the night of the break-in, please contact the Whispering Falls' Sheriff Department.

Be sure to stop by Glorybee Pet Shop to take advantage of the 25% off food for your beloved pets and hair care needs. Remember to have a spiritual day!

The last line of the Whispering Falls Gazette was barely over when the door flung open; Aunt Helena and Eloise shoving each other out of the way to see who could get in first.

"She's my niece!" Aunt Helena raised a finger to Eloise, her eyes staring down it.

I rushed over and pulled it out of the air. Her finger was powerful.

"I just got this place put back together." I huffed and tugged on the tablecloth on one of the display tables next to us.

I didn't have time to wash all the ones that were soaked from the all the broken lotions and cures so I had to dig deep in the storage room for the old ones Darla had used. They were a little musty, but it wasn't anything a few sprits of air freshener wouldn't take care of. I had hoped the wrinkles would fall out, but they didn't.

"You need new coverings." Aunt Helena walked around the shop, touching each table and taking out all the wrinkles.

"Enough of this chit-chat," Eloise said softly, her eyes narrowing. "I'm. . ."

Ahem, Aunt Helena cleared her throat and drummed her fingers together.

"*We*," Eloise emphasized *we*, "are thrilled you and Oscar have agreed to get married on All Hallows Eve since everyone will be here for the festivities, but we are concerned about KJ."

"Not that he isn't capable, but he's a Native American spiritualist and you are not." Aunt Helena couldn't keep her mouth shut long enough for Eloise to get it out. "We," she gestured between the two, "were hoping you would have the Marys do it since it's sort of a royal affair for our families."

"I appreciate all your concern and *we*," I emphasized *we* like Eloise did. "Oscar and I are very happy with our choice. Now," I rushed back to the bubbling cauldron and turned it down.

I ran my finger down the line of potion bottles that were empty and lightly touched each one until the clear cracked liter bottle lit up; which meant it was the perfect bottle for the stress free lotion I was making—minus Darla's wisteria vine oil.

"If you two will excuse me, Faith is going to run the shop while I run some errands." I dipped the ladle into the cauldron and scooped up the yellow mixture, pouring it into the bottle. The yellow liquid turned creamy white as it dripped down into the bottle turning into the lotion.

I grabbed my bag off the chair and stuck the bottle and Madame Torres inside.

"Oscar and I will let you know if we need anything." My brows lifted when I passed them.

"June!" Aunt Helena's voice boomed out, catching my attention. We faced each other. She stuck her hand in her cloak and pulled out a white lace dress. "Since the date is set, I thought you might want this."

"Is that?" I didn't need to ask whom it belonged to. My eyes teared up, my throat dried. I tried to swallow back the lump in my throat. I ran my finger over my engagement ring. My heart warmed. "I had no idea you had Darla's dress."

"I've been waiting until you had a date." She held it out from the hanger.

The ivory cream lace dress was going to be perfect. The ivory lace material lay perfect over the cream silk sheath underneath. The long lace ivory sleeves would be perfect for the cool night weather on All Hallows Eve.

I reached out and ran my hand along the silk collar that ended in the back in a petite silk stiff bow. The zipper up the back ended in keyhole hook and eye closure.

"It's perfect." I even loved the knee length. "Mom was stylish even then." I was afraid to get too close in fear my tears would stain the beautiful dress.

"You are going to look so beautiful." Eloise clasped her hands in front of her face. Her lids were lined with tears. Even Aunt Helena looked choked up.

"Do you mind keeping it until the day because I don't want Oscar to see it." I couldn't stop smiling.

Even though I knew our wedding was far from a traditional wedding, I still wanted to hold some of the tradition I had grown up thinking I was going to have as part of my wedding. The dress was a good place to start.

"I'm sorry you don't believe KJ will be the best fit for our wedding," I put my hands out and with each one took ahold of their hands. "Oscar and I know what we want. And we love KJ like family. He is going to do an amazing job." I squeezed before I let them go and rushed out of the shop.

CHAPTER NINETEEN

On my way out of the shop, I grabbed a section from the wisteria vine and rushed up the hill and jumped into the Green Machine. I had stuck everything in my bag, including some extra smudge sticks, the Magical Cures Book and the clear crackle bottle with the lotion I had made.

KJ had told me to visit the cemetery and that was exactly what I was going to do. Maybe my dream wasn't just a dream of stress, wishing they were here to be with me during the wedding. KJ had put hope in my soul that my parents were trying to get in touch with me from the great beyond.

The cemetery was on spiritual land between Locust Grove and Whispering Falls. No one would know about it unless you were a spiritualist. When Darla had died, it was in her will for her to be buried there. Since we kept to ourselves in Locust Grove, no one but Mac McGurtle and Oscar and his uncle attended the funeral. I never questioned any of Darla's arrangements because I was so distraught at the time—I was in automatic mode.

I pulled off the road into the clearing and got out of the car. The wind blew and the trees parted, making a clear path to the hidden gravesite. There was a black wrought-iron fence around the perimeter of the cemetery with pointy spikes on each stake. A gargoyle sat atop each spike as though it would take off if something were amiss.

I pushed the old gate open but not without a squeak from the hinges. A hoot owl made his presence known from atop the centuries old tree in the middle of the graveyard. The old stones were dotted around the land. Some had moss growing or dangling from them. Most were covered in fresh flowers. Darla and Dad were located in the far right corner of the graveyard. When the wind blew just right, there was a clear view of Whispering Falls to the right and a clear view of Locust Grove on the left.

I'm sure Darla and Dad had picked this spot because they knew I would be living my life between the two towns. They were way wiser about my life than I had been. There was something comforting knowing they could see me wherever I was.

I tiptoed around and over some of the graves to get to Darla and Dad. I didn't want to walk on anyone because it was bad luck and I didn't need any more of that in my life.

Their stone was two round rings intertwined. Their names were chiseled on each of their sides without any dates. When I first saw what Darla had picked out, I thought it was strange she didn't want the dates of birth and of death on there. Now I saw why. The epitaph on their stone read *Eternal life together is never ending.*

I ran my hand around the circles and brushed off the debris.

"I'm sorry I haven't been here in a while." I felt like I needed to talk to them. I sat down cross-legged like I had in my dream and glanced over to the side where my dad had sat in my dream. The space was empty. "There is so much going on. I found out you two played a major hand in my relationship with Oscar." I bit my lip to hold back tears. "Thank you. He is perfect for me and my life. I'm excited to let you know we are going to get married on All Hallows Eve." A warm sensation flowed through my veins, making me believe they were with me. I closed my eyes and took a deep breath.

When I opened them, I looked in the open space next to me and Mr.

Prince Charming was sitting there staring at the stones like my dad had done in my dream.

"How did you know where I was?" I scratched the top of his head. "I thought I got rid of you today," I teased. "Did Petunia not give you enough treats?"

He jumped up and ran to Darla and Dad's tombstone, before jumping up in the circle on Dad's side. He brought his paw up to his face and ran it over his eyes before he started to lick and clean himself.

"Anyway, I'm sure I don't have to tell you what is going on in my life and the craziness of the deal I made with Head To Toe Works."

I took my bag off from around my body and sat it in front of me. I took out Madame Torres and sat her in front of me. She appeared in the globe with a white turban on her head and a big cross in the middle. I took out the vine and sat it next to me along with the Magical Cures Book.

"I can't believe someone broke into the shop and stole the bottle of wisteria vine oil." I picked up the vine and twirled it in my fingers hoping to get some sense of what I needed to do through my intuition. "KJ said I should come here and seek the answers to my problem. Without the bottle, I'm not sure how to get more oil."

The bottles in A Charming Cure were magical and something I couldn't explain. When they were getting low in the ingredients it held, it automatically filled up. If the bottle broke, I was able to get the ingredients, but not this.

"Open the book," Madame Torres floated in a grey pool of water. The waves sloshed up against her face.

As always, I opened the book to the page it was supposed to open to —this time, the recipe for Darla's stress free homeopathic cure. All the ingredients I had put in the lotions were listed; 250 ml (1 cup) of rosewater (or filtered water, or herbal tea), 1 tsp vegetable glycerine, 175 ml (2/3 cup) sunflower oil, 75g (4.5 Tb) coconut oil, 25g. (1/4 cup) beeswax, 20 drops geranium essential oil, 20 drops lavender essential oil, 10 drops patchouli essential oil. Nothing different.

"Lay the vine on the page." Madame Torres's voice was steady, demanding.

I did what she said. The flowers on the vine blew in the wind. The tendrils on the vine glowed a bright green.

"The tendrils." The confirmation that the oils Darla used were in the tendrils flooded my intuition. "Ouch!" I grabbed my wrist and looked down. The liquid was bubbling in the bottle. "Why is it bubbling?" I asked Madame Torres.

Her glass globe glowed with red fire. Her face was gone, but her eyes were lit up with blue streaks flashing through them like bits of lightning. Her globe began to bubble, coming to a rolling boil. Before my eyes, the potion bottle on my charm bracelet burst and sprayed all over the Magical Cures Book.

The words on the page burst out like fireworks. Explosions of letters and words shot in the air, slowly falling down back into the book. Like magic, the Magical Cures Book had transformed. The words were no longer written in Darla's handwriting, but more like calligraphy, fancy writing with potion words only a spiritualist would know.

Mewl, mewl. Mr. Prince Charming howled with his head to the gypsy moon that had covered the cemetery in the broad daylight. The pages of the book flipped fast until the cover shut itself. The moon retreated, Madame Torres's ball went blank, and Mr. Prince Charming was gone. Everything had gone back to normal.

I gathered my stuff and carefully put it all back in my bag. I stood in front of my parents' grave. The sun glittered down on the cemetery illuminating each tomb with a radiant glow.

"I thought you might be here." My heart sang with delight when I heard Oscar's voice behind me. "I called the shop and Faith said you took off but not without grabbing all sorts of stuff."

"I'm glad you found me," I gushed and wrapped my arms around him. "Even from the grave, Darla gave me the secret." I patted my bag that was resting on the side of my body. "The oil comes from the tendrils of the stem and Madame Torres gave me the instructions exactly like she was supposed to."

"And that surprises you?" he asked.

"Yes." I cackled. "She never really does what I need her to do without a hassle."

"Did you talk to them?" He nodded toward the stone.

"I did." Oscar's presence gave me a joy that burrowed deep within me.

Oscar withdrew his arms from around me and bent down on one knee, facing my dad's grave.

"Mr. Heal," Oscar nervously cleared his throat.

"Oscar?" I put my hand on his shoulder. "What are you doing?"

He looked up at me. His gaze was as soft as his touch.

"Mr. Heal, I would like to ask you for your daughter's hand in marriage." His words made my heart ache. My stomach flipped and flopped. "I, we, understand you and my parents really wanted us to get married, but there was no need for you to worry. June is and always has been my first love. She has been my best friend for as long as I have had a memory. There is nothing I want more than to spend the rest of my life next to my best friend. I will keep her warm and safe and forever take care of her."

He stood up and held both my hands up to his lips, kissing both. His eyes scanned me critically and beamed approval when I smiled, blinking a tear from my eye.

"I know I should've done this a long time ago when I asked you, but I didn't know how to get you here." His words were soft spoken and calculated. "June, you have unlocked my heart and soul. I give you my all and am so proud to have you by my side the rest of our lives and call you my wife."

In an instant, the sun beamed down like a flashlight on my parents' stone, the grass around them illuminated greener than the rest of the cemetery, Darla's drowsy daisies popped up in a circle around me and Oscar.

"I guess they approve." He pulled me close to him, softly his breath fanned my face, "I love you, June Heal."

CHAPTER TWENTY

My upcoming wedding to Oscar should've been the first thing on my mind and I was so filled with happiness about how he had shown up at the cemetery and properly asked for my hand in marriage. The response of Mother Earth was a sure sign my parents knew what was going on and were happy for the union.

It should be enough for me to move on, but I knew and my gut told me I couldn't be completely happy without trying to figure out who stole my wisteria vine oil, who killed Burt Rossen, and why.

Oscar was so happy after he proposed again, that I didn't bother telling him about my plan to go to Mac's and pick the bartender's brain about Burt and Tiffany. If Burt had a real hot temper, maybe someone saw it. I understood my product was costing them a little more money and it was a source of stress between them, but not enough to kill.

Oscar decided to go back to Locust Grove police station to interview more employees and I decided to go back to Whispering Falls so I could not only put the finishing touches on the stress free lotion with the new extraction technique, but it was also a top priority to get the Magical Cures Book back in a safe place. With everything going on, I was still excited to open the book and see what new magical potions had been revealed.

The wooden sign on the way into town read, "Welcome to Whispering Falls, A Charming Village." It put a smile on my face and the memory of the first time I had seen it on my first trip to Whispering Falls. All the firsts were flooding my mind. No doubt due to the sentimentality of my upcoming nuptials.

The sidewalks were filled with tourists milling in and out of the shops. Bella stood outside her cream cottage shop. The pink door was a standout from the other shop doors. Not because of the color, all the shops had very colorful gates and entrances only adding to the magical feel of our village. The pink door of Bella's Baubles had the most spectacular jewels imbedded throughout and glistened when the sun or the moon touched it.

I waved when I drove past. There was an empty parking space in front of Magical Moments so I parked there.

"Hello!" I waved to Bella on my way over to talk to her. I held my hand up in the air. She would be so interested in knowing what the liquid from the charm really meant.

"I hear you have set a date," she said, breaking into a wide-open smile exposing the gap between her teeth.

"Oh, Bella," I gushed. "You wouldn't believe what happened today."

"I also heard about the deal falling through." Her face melted into a frown.

"Oh gosh, I'm not worried about that." I hope my pretense of non-concern fooled her. "But Oscar." I crossed my hands over my heart. "He found me at the cemetery and he asked my dad for my hand in marriage."

"Your dad?" She drew back and instantly became wide awake.

"My parents' grave. And he was so sweet. It was magical." I happily sighed and ran my hand over my hair. My bracelet jingled, reminding me of the charm. "And the charm with your Red Devil Smoking Hot incense," I held my arm out in front of me and wagged it side-to-side. "The liquid exploded into the air and all over my Magical Cures Book Darla left me. It was amazing. All the old words completely disappeared and new, real potions not written in Darla's handwriting flew on the pages. The harm to none was right. It's given me so many new ideas to help people out."

The heavy lashes that had created a shadow flew open.

"I couldn't believe it." I shook my head. "I have all new potions to try and customers are going to be so happy. Plus I know how Darla extracted the oil from the wisteria vine."

"All in all, it sounds like you have had a fantastic day." She and I both stepped to the side when a tourist walked up the steps of her shop and entered. "I must go. I'm thinking a diamond is going to sell." Her brows cocked.

The planters hanging on the carriage lights had been changed since this morning. Arabella must have used her magic touch to add in the purple aster with the yellow center, yellow moonshine, and the purple fountain grass. The colorful creations put a skip in my step. All of Whispering Falls was buzzing with tourists and A Charming Cure was not different.

Faith's line was almost out the door.

"Hi, I'm June." I shook hands down the line. I grabbed one of the hand lotions that made hands look and feel younger. I offered the customers a free squirt. "Isn't the smell wonderful?"

All the women in line sniffed the back of their hand where I had put a dot of the lotion. A few of them asked if I wouldn't mind getting them a bottle. Of course I didn't mind.

Faith and I worked like a good team. She would ring them up and I'd package their cures or add a special touch if I needed to. Luckily, most were straight sales. When the line had died down to a few, I disappeared behind the counter with my bag and carefully took out the book and the vine.

"Vrurock, micho, drimoid. Extract the oil from hence the from." I held the tendril over the boiling cauldron. Just as the Magical Cures Book had written it would do, the tendril split into fours, dripping oil into the cauldron. The lotion I had made earlier glowed from the bottle. It was ready to be combined. I uncorked the top and let the lotion slide into the thick frothy liquid, turning into a jade potion. It swirled, cooked, and glowed before the cauldron turned off, letting me know it was finished and the potion was done.

I took a vial from the shelf and let the rest of the oil drip into it from the vine for future use and stuck it in my bag. I knew it would be safe there until we found out who had broken into the shop. Something on the page jumped out at me. I looked down and there were highlighted words. I read it out loud, "Use the true oil for life and death." I reread the words over in my head wondering why it was highlighted.

I turned back to the cauldron where it was filled with the lotion that included the final ingredient I needed to complete the stress free potion that was stolen from me. Using the ladle, the liquid was easily transferred back into the intended bottle.

"Is everything okay?" I poked my head out from behind the partition.

Mr. Prince Charming had found his way back to the shop and sat on the chair behind the counter. Faith was petting him. I swear he had a grin.

CHAPTER TWENTY-ONE

Faith was kind enough to close the shop for me after I told her a lame lie about me having to go to Locust Grove to pick out some wedding things. It was a good excuse to get away without anyone suspecting anything. If I would have told her I was going to Mac's in Locust Grove, she would've told the world.

I had to find out who broke into my shop. And why. And if Pearl and Josh knew something. Sonny said he had heard a lot of employees go there. From what I remember, Tiffany did say she had met Burt there.

"What on earth am I going to wear to a bar?" I asked Mr. Prince Charming who was sitting on my bed watching me throw clothes out of my closet.

My clothes were pretty basic and I never really went too many places to need anything else. I had a couple of black dresses that might be okay. I pulled one hanger off the rod and held it up. It was a bit short for a bar and perfect for a date with Oscar but it was the only thing I really had.

Within minutes, I had the dress on with a pair of black flats, and with a swipe of lipstick was out the door.

"No," I pointed my finger when Mr. Prince Charming appeared next to me by the Green Machine. "I thought I left you inside." My eyes narrowed and my lips pursed.

Rowl! Mr. Prince Charming let out a disgruntled groan and darted down the hill toward Whispering Falls.

On the way to the bar, I had time to go over all of the questions I might have for anyone who might be there. Plus I was on the lookout for someone with long fingernails, like the shadowy figure in a fight with Burt hours before he died. Surely if Mac's was where the employees hung out, they were around Burt much longer and more than I ever was and I'd seen his bad side within eight hours of being around him.

The asphalt parking lot at Mac's had more holes than it did asphalt. The old building had been an old barn that the owner, Mac, had turned into a bar. I recalled when it had come to town and the local news station had done an exposé on how he had rehabbed the old barn instead of tearing it down, but since I wasn't a big bar hopper or drinker, I never had gone to the place, so it was a good night to check it out.

"June, June," the night wind whispered my name causing me to jump.

"Hello?" I called into the darkness around me. Mac sure could use some outside lighting besides the large barn light above the loft door that I had to bet was there for pure aesthetics.

"Psst." The voice called, "Over here."

My eyes squinted as I glanced around the dark to see. At the corner of the barn I saw a white furry tail swaying in the darkness.

"Mr. Prince Charming?" I asked and he ran over to me.

Amethyst Plum walked around the corner of the barn where my ornery cat had appeared. Her black hair was braided in a fishtail and ran down her back. Her thick brows, dark eyes, and long lashes were covered in the smoky eye look. She wore a pair of black pencil thin pants, tapered at the ankle, a grey ruffle sleeveless blouse and a pair of grey flats.

"You naughty cat." I picked him up to reprimand him for getting Amethyst to come to Mac's.

"He insisted," Amethyst said and met me halfway. "Not only that, but I had a really bad dream about an old lady and it has to do with you."

"Old lady." I knew she had to be talking about Jenny Rossen because she was the only old lady associated with everything going on in my life that seemed to be the glue to all this Head To Toe Works mess.

"There is danger around her and when Mr. Prince Charming came to Full Moon tonight, I knew something was wrong and followed him here." She glanced sharply around, her eyes ablaze. "There is deep-seated evil around here and I'm worried."

"We will be fine." The last thing I needed was a bit of fear to bring down the confidence I had built up on the way over here.

"And the Marys were looking for you." Her eyes darted about the darkness.

The light streaming out of the front door of Mac's caused us both to look when it opened and a couple drunks stumbled out.

"I have to go in there." I dragged the toe of my flat along a chipped piece of asphalt. "I know someone from Head To Toe Works broke into my shop and stole Darla's last homeopathic cure I owned. I also know they are the sole reason my product was pulled out of the company. I promised the Village Council they could have part of the money from the sales and I want to make good on my promise."

"Sometimes we can't help if things go wrong. Just because we are of the spiritual world, it doesn't mean we can fix things that shouldn't be fixed or we can change the course of the universe." Amethyst always had wise words.

"I understand my product might not be meant for the world to use because of our real gift, but that still doesn't mean someone has the right to steal from me either." I completely understood what Amethyst was saying, but it was the last real cure I had from Darla and it was something I cherished.

"Then we will figure out who took the cure from your store, but as for the murder, I think you need to leave that up to Oscar and the police because something very evil lurks there." The look in her eyes caused me to pause.

Though I didn't agree, I didn't disagree either.

The door swung open again with more people spilling out into the parking lot, laughing and telling stories. Honky-tonk music blared from within and I could see some line dancing in the back of the bar.

"I'm going in. You are more than welcome to come with me," I invited Amethyst but didn't wait to see if she was coming.

There was a lot of hooting and hollering coming from the dance floor. None other than Josh and a few other faces I had recognized but not talked to from Head To Toe Works were leading the boot-scootin' crowd.

"Now what?" Amethyst's brows rose.

"There." I pointed to the two empty barstools that happened to be next to Ronald, the security guard who had given me such a hard time on my first day of work at the factory.

We moseyed up and took a seat like we knew what we were doing. My stomach knotted, sending my intuition on high alert.

"It's you," Ronald's face contorted when he saw me.

The frost from his mug dripped, leaving a puddle on the wooden bar. His tired eyes bore into me and there was stubble around his jaw line.

"I've never seen you here before." The lines around his eyes creased even deeper making him look much older than he really was.

"I had heard everyone from work comes here so me and my friend," I gestured to Amethyst next to me, "thought we might stop in for a drink."

"What'll you have?" he asked and downed what was left in his mug.

He sat it down in the puddle and lifted his finger in the air. The bartender came over, picked up the mug, tossing it in the steamy water behind the bar.

"Another one." Ronald said when the bartender wiped down the counter in front of him. "And whatever they are drinking."

"Don't you think you've had enough?" The bartender paid no attention to me. "You've been here all day."

"You either want my money or not," Ronald growled and glared at the man.

"What do you ladies want?" The bartender threw cocktail napkins in front of us.

"I'll have a Coke." Amethyst smiled.

"I'll have the same." I smiled.

"You come to a bar and have a Coke?" Ronald's words were biting. He chuckled nastily. "You could've gone to McDonald's for that." His head swung around my way. "What is it you really want?"

"You see, my friend June," Amethyst got off her stool and stood in the small space between me and Ronald. "Really wanted to sell her product through the company and we just don't know why it folded. We thought maybe a big guy like you could give us a little insight."

Starting from his shoulder, Amethyst dragged her long nail down his arm and stopped at his big hands. She tapped this wrist.

"You sure have nice strong hands." She grinned. Inwardly I groaned and I rolled my eyes.

Ronald seemed to be taken by it as his eyes watched Amethyst's finger make small circles across his hand.

"Darlin', you don't know the half of it." His lips curled at the edges.

"Then why don't you tell me," she whispered in his ear loud enough for me to hear.

If I'd known Amethyst was this good with guys, I would've included her a long time ago. My gut told me Mr. Prince Charming knew what he was doing when he went to the Treesort to get her tonight. Good fairy-god cat, my insides smiled.

"I don't know why someone would kill Burt. He was a good guy. Always was." Ronald's voice broke. "I've known him all my life. He met Tiffany right over there." He pointed across the bar to a group of college age kids who were enjoying a round of shots. Their laughter filled the bar. "She woo'ed him right out of his momma's house. Bless her heart."

"His momma?" I pushed Amethyst out of the way to probe for more. "Sorry, Amethyst."

"Yeah, sweetie." Amethyst winked at him. Her long lashes drew down and back up. I could practically hear his heart palpitation from her flirting with him. "What about his momma?"

"She is a good woman. She loves her son so much and was naturally leery when Tiffany came around throwing her money in Burt's face." Ronald had an awe-shucks look on his face. "He had never been married or had kids, but he had a promising career with a large marketing firm up in Lexington. Tiffany talked him right out of it and right in her bed."

"And that's bad?" Amethyst was really playing the part as she rubbed her hand on his back.

"When your momma who has loved you and taken care of you all your life is left out in the cold because of a few romps in the bed, I'd say that qualifies for bad." Ronald reached around and patted Amethyst's hand. She drew it back from him and placed it on his leg.

"Do you think his momma would've been angry enough with her son to kill him?" Amethyst went for the throat with her words.

Her frankness didn't seem to bother Ronald because he leaned way over the bar, her ruffles falling to the side to give him a good look at her chest. She grabbed her Coke and took a nice long seductive drink, her eyes never leaving Ronald's.

"Ahhh. . ." she sighed, licking her lips.

"Um. . ." Ronald babbled.

Again, I rolled my eyes.

"Yeah, would she kill him?" I interrupted.

"Nah." He shook his head and took another sip of his beer. "Though there was a time when Burt went to see his momma because Tiffany was going to make him. . ."

"Hey! I thought that was you!" Josh stumbled up between us and practically knocked Ronald out of the way.

"Josh, you are interrupting." I tried to shove him back. I had to hear what Ronald was going to say. It could have been a big piece of information about why Jenny might have a motive.

"Hey old man." Josh smacked Ronald on the back. He grabbed my hand. "Let's dance. You probably need practice before that big day of yours."

There was no protesting because his tattooed hand dragged me out on the dance floor in the middle of the dancers twirling, whirling, stepping to each side before shimmying down to the ground. It was like they had all taken the same dance class.

"Watch it!" Someone shoved me when I bumped into them.

"Hey!" The person on the other side of me screamed after I stepped on their toe when I didn't shuffle to the right with the rest of the crowd.

I shimmied the best I could as my eyes watched Ronald and Amethyst in the distance leaving the bar. She sure was a good friend; I knew she was going to pump him for information about Jenny and Tiffany. One of them had to have broken into my shop.

While she did that, I knew I could sneak around and ask about the murder.

With a break in the music, I hurried my way off the dance floor while Josh was talking to another group of people and sat back down on my stool.

"Another Coke?" the bartender asked.

"No thanks." I waved him off.

"So, you and your friend seem to be asking a lot of questions about Burt Rossen." His face colored with uneasiness. "I don't want no trouble here. Like I told the cops, the Rossens might have bought this bar out from under me, but I'm not ratting them out."

"They own this bar?" I asked.

He nodded. "I was having some financial difficulty about five years ago and sought out a marketing firm in Lexington to help me. Burt came in and he had the best ideas. Only I couldn't make his business plan a reality because of the cost in doing so. He wheeled his momma in here one day and she took a look around and they offered to be partners. They own the majority, which I guess Tiffany and Jenny do now, and I keep running the place."

"It looks like you are doing well. Can't you buy them out?" I asked.

"It's not Jenny. Tiffany wouldn't let it happen." He went over to the rowdy crowd across the bar when they hollered for him.

Across the bar, I noticed Josh talking to someone. It was Pearl. He pointed toward me and she looked over. I gave her a big wave, but she ignored me and took off out the door.

"Pearl!" I tried to sling my bag over my shoulder as I rushed out of Mac's after her. "Pearl!" I yelled. "Wait!"

"What do you want?" She turned, her eyes conveyed the fury within her.

"I wanted to talk to you about the factory," I said and noticed the snarl on her face. "Listen, I'm sorry the factory was shut down but it wasn't because of me."

"I never said it was and it's not like we are friends. I met you a couple of times," she said through gritted teeth.

"I get the feeling there is more to it than that." I put a hand on her shoulder and got a jolt.

My intuition told me she was having an inner battle with loyalty. Her nerves were standing on end. I sucked in a deep breath and had to use my other hand to physically pull my hand off her.

"I can help you if you are battling something," I assured her.

"Don't go and use that voodoo crap on me." She folded her arms across her chest. I noticed her white shirt had a logo on it.

"I see you got another job." I pointed.

"What's it of your concern?" she asked.

"Locust Grove Convalescent Home?" I questioned the logo of the home with a heart in the attic portion of the photo.

"It's an old folks home. My mom lives there and they just so happened to have an opening in the cleaning crew." There was bridled anger in her voice. "Did you know that I hate cleaning?"

"I don't know anyone who doesn't." I laughed and tried to break the ice between us.

"Listen, I think you are a nice enough person and all, but we come from two different worlds." She gestured between us. "This is as far as we go. Understand?"

"Understand." A surge of urgency to agree with her hit me.

She knew a lot more than she wanted me to know. It was exactly what Faith had said about Pearl or Josh knowing something about the break-in. Now I had narrowed it down.

Pearl.

When I got into the Green Machine to head back to Whispering Falls, Mr. Prince Charming was already curled up on the dashboard sound asleep.

He lifted his head, yawned and put his head back down. His eyes focused on me.

"One thing is for sure." I watched the taillights of Pearl's car fade off around the curve of the old road in the darkness. "Pearl knows more than she's letting on and it's up to me to find out."

Mr. Prince Charming purred happily as I started the car. I was a little concerned about Amethyst, but before I went out to the dance floor, she'd insisted she wanted to hang out with Ronald a little more.

I glanced over at Mr. Prince Charming and swore he had a smile on his face. He seemed to always be the happiest when we made our way back to Whispering Falls. As did my heart and soul. It was home. A place of protection. And I needed to feel safe with the thief behind bars. And I couldn't help but think the thief and the murderer were one and the same. My gut told me Pearl held the key.

CHAPTER TWENTY-TWO

The phone chirped on my bedside table waking me up from a deep sleep. I grabbed it without looking to see who was calling me in the middle of the night.

"June?" Oscar's voice questioned from the other end of the line. "Are you okay?"

"Are you okay?" My heart skipped a beat. I bolted up out of bed to find Madame Torres staring at me from her ball as she was sitting on my dresser and Mr. Prince Charming was sitting on the pillow next to me staring.

"Everyone is a little worried since you weren't there to open the shop so I went ahead and let Faith in before I went to Locust Grove." His voice was concerned.

"What time is it?" I glanced over at the clock and couldn't believe it was almost ten in the morning. "Oh no."

"I was on my way up to your house to check on you around seven a.m., and I passed Amethyst coming down the hill." He knew.

I closed my eyes and gulped. Oscar was not going to be happy that I had gone to a bar, much less nosed around about the break-in and murder.

"Oh," I managed not to go into a begging plea.

"And after she said the two of you went out for a drink at Mac's, I decided to let you sleep." Oscar fell silent.

"Thank you." I waited.

"I didn't realize you liked going to bars," Oscar said sarcastically. "I mean, if this wedding stuff is really stressing you out, then maybe we shouldn't get married."

"No, no, no." I got out of bed and headed to the kitchen. I grabbed a mug out of the cupboard and poured a cup of coffee, thankful for the timer set every day for my coffee to be ready when I woke. "That's not it at all."

"Then what is it?" he asked. "You've been acting so weird. Even Sonny said you came into the station. Do you have something you need to tell me?"

"No." I took a sip and decided to keep the information to myself about the will and the stuff I had felt about Pearl until I could go to the nursing home myself and talk to her again. "Amethyst and I just wanted to have some girl time. Like a bachelorette party."

I was thankful Amethyst didn't spill her guts.

"But the wedding is a few months away and don't those happen a week before the wedding?" Oscar was digging.

I held to my guns. There was nothing pressing to tell him. Burt wasn't going to come back alive. Whoever broke into my shop stole the only bottle of the wisteria vine oil I had and they had no way of knowing I had made more. Everything in my gut felt safe. . .for now.

"I'll do that with all the girls. You know Amethyst and I got off on the wrong foot and she's offered us a honeymoon tree cabin for our wedding night." I quickly regretted my lie, but thought it was a good idea, so visiting Amethyst to thank her for not telling Oscar the truth while asking her for a room was first on my list. Even before visiting Pearl at the nursing home.

It was true. When Amethyst came to town, I had accused her of some really evil stuff that wasn't true. She turned out to be a really great spiritualist and last night proved it.

"Did you say Faith was okay with working?" I asked.

"She said she had nothing else to do," he confirmed. "Hey, why don't you meet me after my shift tonight and let me take you on a date?"

"Great! I'd love to." It was the perfect ending to our conversation in what could have turned out bad, if I would have spilled my guts about the real reason I had gone to the bar.

Oscar might be suspicious, and I was okay with that. I'd tell him the truth soon enough.

CHAPTER TWENTY-THREE

One would never know the massive structure of Full Moon Treesort, Whispering Falls' only bed and breakfast, was nestled deep within the woods behind our village. The double-decker A-frame structure was nothing but windows that overlooked the most spectacular views Whispering Falls had to offer.

It wasn't your typical bed and breakfast where the rooms were in one building. The Full Moon Treesort rooms were scattered among the trees in the forest. Each one had a different theme, a different view, and a different purpose for the customer. Amethyst didn't let the customer pick the room they wanted. Her gift of Onerirocriticy; dream interpretation, helped her. She told me once that she had a dream of all her clients and knew exactly what they needed from her before they even got there.

I had yet to see any one of her clients walk away not loving the Treesort and not booking another stay. She was filled to the gills and I hoped I wasn't too late in getting something for my honeymoon.

"Good morning, June!" Her voice called before I made it up the steps of the main lodge.

The homemade smell of freshly baked blueberry muffins wafted out of the lodge and throughout the woods.

"You are just in time for breakfast." She held a coffee pot above a couple cups and poured. "Although it is almost time for lunch."

She hummed happily as I took a seat. Her hair was taken out of the fishtail braid and lay in loose curls around her back. Her eyes were wide awake and alive. Not at all how mine looked. There was a giggle to her upward smile and her dark eyes danced under her perfectly trimmed thick brows.

"You are awfully chipper this morning. Whereas Oscar woke me up with a phone call." I held the cup up to my nose and took a nice long inhale. The brew was strong and swirled out of the cup and hugged my nose. "I want to thank you for not telling Oscar about last night."

"It was a lot of fun." Ronald rounded the corner and gave Amethyst a swift smack on her bottom.

My jaw dropped and I nearly let go of the cup.

Ronald was clean shaven, his hair nicely combed and a fresh set of clothes made him look like a million bucks.

"Yes it was." Amethyst cocked her right brow, her lip followed. She lifted the cup to her lips and took a sip. Ronald nipped at her neck. She placed her free hand on his head and let out a little giggle.

My gut dropped. What had I done? Didn't Amethyst know how hard it was to date a mortal? Someone not from our spiritual world?

"Ronnie, dear." Amethyst set her cup down. "Why don't you be a good little boy and take this tray to Dreamy Sleep cabin for me."

"Roar," Ronald held his hand up like a claw and growled at her. He took the tray and walked out.

"Are you joking me?" I asked. "I really thought you were putting on an act last night with all the rubbing and touching."

"I was until I met the animal in him and you know I can't resist a good animal." Her grin was evil. "Not to mention I need a date for an upcoming wedding." She winked.

"Which reminds me," I was going to ask her about that honeymoon room.

"Of course you can stay in the Lover's Nest on your honeymoon. My treat." She drummed her fingers on the counter.

"No, I will pay," I assured her.

"Not if I get my way with Ronnie." This time her grin reached her eyes. "He just might be the one."

"Oh, Amethyst. It's so hard to be married to a mortal." I knew it wasn't my place to beg her to rethink what she was feeling, but I felt like I had to since I had gotten her into this mess.

"He's handy." She curled her hand into the air as if she were summoning magic. "He can do things without our little gift and what he doesn't know won't hurt him. Plus wasn't that how you were brought up?"

"It was, but my dad had died before I knew better." I bit the inside of my lip. "Do me a favor and ask Eloise how hard it was for my mom to live within the community. Eloise was not part of Whispering Falls. She had to live in the woods because she was a Dark-Sider with a Good-Sider family. She let my mom in on her little secret and they had formed a partnership and friendship."

Amethyst took in everything I was saying; I just hoped it was sinking in.

"So ask her how my mom felt and dealt with it." I suggested. It was all I could do.

The love in Amethyst's heart radiated out of her and she had fallen hard for Ronald. . .um Ronnie. . .in just a few hours.

"I guess you'd be interested in what I got out of him when I promised him some naughty things." Her face glowed.

"First off, I don't want to know about any naughty things, but I'm definitely interested if he said something about the factory." I leaned in.

"He said things started getting real sticky after about a year of marriage between Burt and Tiffany. Burt started to fall into the rich mantraps and lifestyle Tiffany's company had offered." She looked over her shoulder. The coast was clear. "He had bought into Mac's before he married Tiffany. She started going there more and more trying to get these high dollar wines included on the menu, but Mac refused. Ronnie said it was a mess."

"So Tiffany was controlling the situation?" I asked. It was hard to believe it since I had seen him grab her.

"Up until the deal was made with you." Her cheeks balled on her face. "Ronnie said that after they came back from here, Tiffany cowed down to Burt on a few occasions, but I'm not sure why because then he sort of passed out."

"You ladies aren't gossiping about me are you?" Ronald walked into the large gathering space where the kitchen was. He was followed by a couple of Full Moon's guests.

"Of course we are." Amethyst winked and kissed his cheek.

"Thanks for the coffee," I got up, "and especially for the room."

My heart felt like it was laughing and dancing within. The thought of spending a romantic night after my wedding with Oscar put me on cloud nine. I put that feeling deep in the back of my heart. I knew I would have to solve this crime before I could enjoy any more wedding plans. With Faith running the shop, I knew my first stop had to be Mac's.

I had a few questions I needed to ask him.

CHAPTER TWENTY-FOUR

I probably should've gone to check on Faith, but I had left the shop fully stocked and I trusted her completely. Plus she had my cell phone in case she had an emergency in addition to a full village of people who would come to her aid if she needed it.

Mac's looked a lot different in the daylight and I could see where Tiffany would want to spruce it up a bit.

I pulled up and parked the Green Machine up to the front next to the only other car in the lot. I opened the door of the bar. Mac knew more than he was telling me last night and I wanted to hear the history between him, Burt and Burt's mother.

"Sorry! We are closed." Mac, the bartender, was crouched down behind the bar.

The bar top was lined with cardboard boxes.

"Putting away your liquor shipment?" I asked.

He stood up. His eyes were bloodshot.

"Shipment?" He scoffed. "Packing up for good."

"For good?" I asked.

"Listen, Nancy Drew," Mac planted his hands on the bar. "Mac's is closed. Forever."

"Why?" I questioned.

"Now that Burt is gone, his will was read and I'm no longer the majority share holder, so she shut me down." He shook his head and grabbed a box, taking it out the door.

I followed him.

"Can she do that?" I asked. This Jenny Rossen was a real pain in a lot of people's lives.

"When you are the majority shareholder, you can do anything." He threw the box in the car and walked back in, leaving me outside.

The only person I knew I had to see was Pearl. Faith all but confirmed that Pearl knew something and when I touched her last night, I knew she was the one I needed to talk to.

Growing up in Locust Grove, you heard about the old folks' home, but never went unless you were part of a Girl Scouts group or church group. Darla didn't let me participate in those types of activities, but Oscar's Uncle Jordan did.

Long story short, Oscar's Uncle Jordan raised him and did so in a way Oscar wouldn't find out he was a spiritualist. Jordan was against our heritage. So much so, he was the one who ended up killing my father along with Oscar's parents, sending Jordan to prison. Still, he did take Oscar to church groups and tried to get Oscar to be part of groups like the Boy Scouts, making me very envious for their life of normalcy.

The Locust Grove Convalescent Home sat on a hundred acres in the country. Tall oak trees lined the long drive, giving shade to the cars underneath. The red building was adorned and decorated with large cement molds of fleur-de-lis along the circumference of the roof. In the distance were several small cottage homes, all looking the same, with a tiny porch on the front only big enough for one rocking chair. I had heard those were for elders who could live on their own until it was time that they no longer could and moved into the communal living area.

I pulled into the parking lot, found one of the visitor spots and parked. When I got out, I looked around. On the side of the building was a covered outdoor patio where it looked as if some of the residents were playing cards, shuffleboard and ping pong. To the left of the building there was a pool dotted with elders wearing blue water caps. They were lifting their arms in the air following a much younger woman in the front.

"Can I help you?" A woman with a garden cart walked by. She was older and had a floppy hat with a drawstring tightly snugged around her chin. Her thin long-sleeved white shirt helped ward off the heat of the summer sun. She wore capris and a pair of those plastic shoes with holes all over them. She leaned on the cart that was filled with potting soil, gardening tools, and a potted Gerbera daisy. "You look to be lost. New for sure."

"I'm looking for the office." I had suddenly realized I had no idea what was Pearl's last name.

"Thataway." She pointed her gloved finger in the direction of the building. "I best be on my way if I'm going to make it over to Jenny's before five o'clock."

"Jenny?" I asked wondering the odds of it being the Jenny I was looking for.

"Jenny Rossen. She insists she gets her daisy before five o'clock. Persnickety she is." The old woman used the back of her hand to push the hat up from over top her eyes. "If I'm gonna make it there by then," she looked at her watch, "I better get going."

"It's only three o'clock." I glanced at the potted flower.

"You see all them people?" Her hand waved in front of us at the patio and the pool. I nodded. "I'm pretty popular around here so I have to say my hellos when I pass. I can't be a snob."

"Oh, of course not," I said with a smile.

She was cute and social. It made me wonder what type of grand-motherly figure Darla would've been. Definitely the hippy type any child would love and connect with.

"Listen," I leaned in. "I'm friends with Burt, Jenny's son, and that is exactly who I came to visit. Why don't you give me her cottage number and the flower and I'll take it to her."

"Oh, I don't know." The woman shook her head. "It's part of my job."

"But every night? Don't you want a night off when I'm going over to see her anyway?" I did my best sweet-talking.

"Well," she picked up the pot and handed it to me. "I'd love to be able to participate in the beginning of water aerobics at four-thirty. Because of Jenny's daisy I'm always twenty minutes late."

She pulled back the shoulder of her white shirt and showed me the bathing suit strap underneath.

"Great. You enjoy your class." I held the pot close to me. "Which cottage is hers?"

"Cottage? Burt didn't tell you?" The woman's lips turned down. "Well, I'll keep my mouth shut. She's not in a cottage. Jenny was moved to assisted living over a year ago. Room 214."

"Assisted living?" My head clouded over. Were Burt and Jenny snowing people over? What was going on? There was only one way to find out. Head to room 214.

I didn't have to use my witchy gift to realize room 214 was located on the second floor. And since I had flowers, no one questioned who I was or why I was there.

The plaque on the wall pointed me right according to the numbers of the room. The red carpet had gold diamonds dotted throughout. Some of the doors had wreaths while others had nothing. Next to the room numbers were their names. Room 214 was bare and it made me sad. I knew if Darla was somewhere like this, I would make sure she had fresh flowers and a wreath.

At least Jenny had the flowers.

I knocked on the slightly open door.

"Come on in, Ida." An elderly voice called from behind the door. "You are early today."

I stepped inside and opened my mouth. Nothing came out when I realized Jenny Rossen was a very petite grey-headed woman who wore a house dress and used a cane. A blind person's cane. She tapped the edge of the cane on the floor and shuffled her house-shoed feet across the room.

"What beautiful color did Burt send today?" she asked.

"Um. . ." There was a lump in my throat. There was no way this woman had anything to do with Burt's death nor did she even know he was dead.

"Purple, Ms. Rossen. A beautiful purple Gerbera daisy." Pearl swooped in and grabbed the pot from me.

"Pearl is that you? Where is Ida?" She was confused.

Pearl put the pot in front of Jenny and took her hand, placing it on the clay exterior.

"She decided to do water aerobics early tonight. She will be back tomorrow." Pearl turned her head and glared at me.

Jenny cocked her head to the side with a blank stare my way.

"Pearl, is someone else in the room?" Jenny asked.

"Yes, ma'am." I spoke up, ignoring Pearl's evil glare. "I'm June Heal." I took a lotion from my bag and walked over to them.

"June, from the new product line Burt has told me about?" Jenny questioned.

"Yes, ma'am." Pearl stepped away with the planter tucked in her arms and let me put my lotion out in front of me. "Here." I took Jenny's hand and placed it on the ornamental bottle.

The bottle glowed. Pearl stepped back. Her eyes as big as saucers. I leaned my head back. The pain in my heart was almost too great for me to bear. The stress free lotion was channeling all the pain Jenny Rossen was going to feel when she found out Burt had been murdered.

"June?" Jenny broke the jolt of energy digging into my soul.

"I. . ." A tear broke out of my eye and down my cheek.

"I think it's time for Ms. Rossen to have her dinner. If you don't mind, Ms. Heal, visiting hours are over." Pearl stepped up and took the lotion from me. "I'll be sure to give Jenny some of this fine lotion you have left for her."

Pearl's words stung. Faith's words hit me. Pearl? Was Pearl the killer?

"Pearl, how is your momma?" Jenny asked. "I haven't heard her laugh in a couple of days."

"She's fine, Ms. Rossen. I'll be sure to tell her to stop by and see you when she's on her way down to bingo." Pearl took Jenny by the arm and led her over to her bed. "Ms. Rossen, you take your afternoon nap and I'll put the Gerbera on the windowsill for it to get a little sunshine while you rest your eyes."

"June, aren't you going to say goodbye?" Jenny held her arms out as her legs dangled from the side of the bed. "I'm so glad you are here. Burt told me you were working hard. I don't know why on earth he ever wanted to buy a company that sold women's lotions. Especially since he's never left home or been married."

"Now you rest." Pearl laid a blanket over Jenny and turned back to me.

Before I could ask Jenny what she meant by saying Burt was never married and he owned Head To Toe Works, Pearl had dragged me out of the room, her fingernails dug deep into my skin, leaving little indentions when she let go.

"What are you doing here?" Pearl questioned. "That woman is fragile. As if you didn't see for yourself. And what was wrong with that bottle?"

"You need to tell me everything you know. Who broke into my store and who killed Burt Rossen?" I ignored her question and asked my own questions.

"I'm not telling you nothing!" She put her finger in my face. "I have a good gig going here with my momma and you ain't going to ruin it. Do you understand me?"

She grabbed me when we heard the elevator doors open and none other than Tiffany Rossen stepped out. Pearl jerked me around the corner and planted herself up against the wall.

"What is she doing here?" Pearl asked with a trembling voice. "This is not good."

"Pearl, what is going on? There is no time to pretend you don't know something," I said in an urgent voice.

"Mr. Burt owned this place when he met that witch of a woman, Tiffany, at the bar that night." She spoke fast. "They had a one-night stand and she came here looking for him, ranting and raving how he got her pregnant and he was going to make an honest woman out of her. Ms. Rossen is so sweet and kind, she would've died if she knew Tiffany and her flashy ways, so Mr. Burt kept his momma a secret from Tiffany all this time."

"How do you know all of this?" I asked.

"I have a degree in accounting and I was the onsite accountant here. I kept the books," Pearl said.

"None of this makes sense." I had heard of some crazy and off-the-wall things in my life, but this took the cake. "You left a good job here to work on the factory line?"

"That ain't the half of it." She pulled me closer after she took another look around the corner. "When Tiffany couldn't get her little lotion company off the ground," she quieted.

"Tell me, Pearl." I knew this was the part I needed to hear.

"I was in my office in the administration building going through the books and something was off. The numbers weren't adding up. Of course we were off a few dollars here and there but when it became thousands of dollars a month, I knew they were cooking the books to pay for her little lotion company."

"Cooking the books?" I tried to follow her as close as I could but I just didn't understand.

"Tiffany wanted her lotion company to do well, so she made Burt take from the old people. Their money. Changing their wills for Tiffany and Burt to become the beneficiaries." Pearl gulped. "When I confronted them, Tiffany said they wouldn't hurt my momma since my momma lived here and then they demoted me to that factory. If I didn't keep my mouth shut, Tiffany threatened to price my momma out of here and I just couldn't afford to put her anywhere else making factory money. As long as I kept my mouth shut, they would take good care of momma."

"What about Mac?" I rolled my hand in front of me to hurry her up. My gut told me time was of the essence.

"Tiffany had gone in and bought that bar right underneath Mac." She shook her head.

"The woman." I gasped remembering what Mac had said. "Mac said something about a woman, but I thought he was talking about Jenny."

"Well, Mr. Burt had a lawyer come here and he changed his will without telling Tiffany. He made his momma the beneficiary of the company. I was here visiting my momma and he dragged me in to be a witness. He said he trusted me." There were tears forming in her eyes. I felt sorry for the pain she was in. "He said that Tiffany had gone crazy when she found out he changed the will because the paralegal from the law office didn't know better and sent the papers to the house."

"And that is how she found out about Jenny?"

"No." Pearl shook her head. "She found out about Jenny when the Gerbera pot bill he sends his momma came to the house. It was around Christmas. Tiffany showed up here with these deviled eggs and nearly killed poor Ms. Rossen." Pearl's eyes grew. "I think she put poison in them."

"Jenny never found out about Tiffany being her daughter-in-law?" I asked.

"Never. Burt said he didn't care if he went to jail. Over his dead body would she meet his momma because his momma couldn't take the stress Tiffany had put him through." Pearl jumped when we heard a scream coming down the hall in the direction of Jenny Rossen's room.

CHAPTER TWENTY-FIVE

Pearl and I rushed back down the hall and tried to open the door but it was locked.

"Burt never locked the door because Ms. Rossen has been blind for as long as I have known her and he wanted to make sure she could get out in an emergency." Pearl beat on the door.

"Help!" The faint cry of the little old lady was heard from underneath the door.

I grabbed the handle and tugged.

"Pearl, I'm going to ask you to turn your head and close your ears." I wasn't about to take no for an answer. When I saw she did what I asked, I grabbed the handle and channeled all of my energy into the handle to open it. I knew it would take all of my energy, but it was worth saving a life.

With the handle hot under my hand, the door flew off the hinges, sending me and Pearl to the ground.

Pearl looked at me with fear in her eyes but didn't say a word as she got up.

Tiffany Rossen was standing over Jenny Rossen with a bed pillow stuck across Jenny's face. Jenny's legs were shaking, her hands gripped the edges of the pillow but she wasn't strong enough to get Tiffany off of her.

"Get off of her!" Pearl grabbed Tiffany by the backs of her arms and wrangled her to the ground.

Like a caged animal, Tiffany clawed Pearl with the longest nails I had ever seen. The two of them wrestled around while I went to Jenny's bedside. Jenny was unconscious but still alive.

"Use the oil in life and death." The highlighted words came out of my mouth without me even thinking about it.

I grabbed the vial of wisteria vine oil out of my purse and quickly unscrewed the lid, letting two drops fall on Jenny's thin lips. Small bursts of fireworks popped over her eyes, they began to flutter. A loud boom shook the room and Jenny sat straight up.

"What is going on? Ida, is that you?" Jenny asked.

"No, Ms. Rossen. It's Pearl." Pearl's body was lying across Tiffany Rossen's and her hand was held tight over Tiffany's mouth, keeping her from speaking. "My friend, June is going to take you for a nice walk. It's beautiful out."

With what little energy I had left, I did exactly what Pearl told me to do because I heard sirens in the background and I knew help was on the way. Plus Pearl had Tiffany Rossen under control.

On my way out the door, I grabbed the tie off of Jenny's robe and tossed it to Pearl. In no time, Pearl had Tiffany hog-tied and ready to go once the police got there.

"I'll take over from here." Ida found me and Jenny in the memorial garden.

Jenny had told me stories how she had bought the nursing home with her husband, Burt's dad, a long time ago and how much he would be proud of his son. I didn't have the heart to even begin to tell her about Burt and what had transpired between him and Tiffany.

If what Pearl had said was true, it would devastate Jenny.

"Ida, you have got to see the Gerbera Burt sent me today." Jenny took Ida's arm and let Ida guide her through the garden.

"I have to tell you something, Jenny." Ida's voice was soft and caring. She was the perfect person to tell Jenny about Burt.

I left them alone and walked back up to the scene of the crime to find Oscar taking Pearl's statement. After he was done, he asked Pearl not to leave the county in case they needed to ask her more questions, but we both knew that meant she might have charges brought against her since she did know about the will, the embezzlement, and the murder of Burt.

"I guess you stuck your nose in the right place this time." Oscar drew me to him. "You could've been hurt, June."

"I know, but I wasn't." I patted him on the back and pulled away. "What happened to Tiffany?"

"Pearl had her tied up and told us everything. Tiffany couldn't protest because Sonny had built a case against her." Oscar pointed toward Sonny.

He waved over at us.

"But I thought Sonny said she was cleared." I recalled him telling me that the day he told me I was cleared.

"She was until we found out she had been getting her nails done and the scrapes on Burt's neck had traces of acrylic. He started digging deeper into Burt's background, finances, all the things we needed warrants for and just put two and two together," Oscar said. "Tiffany told me how Burt kept her a secret from his mother and how he had changed his will over the past week leaving all of his wealth to his mom. He had even cashed in his retirement to pay back all the money he had stolen from the elderly. When everything started piling up that he was going to leave her, she killed him out of rage. She knew she was going to have to make a go of the factory on her own and Gentle June's was her ticket, but only without you, so she stole the bottles she saw you use during her Christmas visit to Whispering Falls."

"So she did break in to A Charming Cure." I could barely wrap my head around everything she had confessed to.

From the beginning she had lied to me. My intuition wasn't wrong at Christmas. It told me she was having family problems with her mother-in-law. Hiding a poison in deviled eggs was her idea. Stress was stress and the secret potion worked differently for everyone. And the nails. She lied about not having them, meaning the shadowy figure Madame Torres showed me was her the entire time.

"What about Mac's? Does Tiffany really have the right to shut him down?" I asked, concerned with Mac's future.

"All of that will have to be straightened out in time." Oscar looked over at the door.

Ida was bringing a heartbroken and sobbing Jenny Rossen back to the room. I picked up the stress lotion I had brought her and gave it to Oscar.

"When you talk to her, put some of this in your hands and hold hers, rubbing the lotion in. It will help her." I watched in sadness as Ida and Pearl helped Jenny sit on the edge of the bed. Jenny clung to Pearl.

CHAPTER TWENTY-SIX

"Cheers!" The clink of glasses filled the barn and the music blared as Josh led the Whispering Falls group out on the dance floor.

"I don't know what to say," Mac said and put Jenny Rossen's hand around a tall glass of sweet tea.

"I don't want you to say anything. You deserve your bar." Jenny had been going around Locust Grove making up for the bad Tiffany had Burt do over the years. She wanted the book thrown at Tiffany for the life she had stolen away from her son.

Jenny sold Head To Toe Works to an international company with a similar name, using the money to pay back anyone Burt and Tiffany had wronged. Burt had left a note in his will to be read only to his mother where he apologized and laid out everything he had done because of Tiffany. He had every account they had embezzled from and Jenny used the sale proceeds from the factory to pay back those debts. She kept the nursing home and made Pearl the head administrator and added Josh to the employee list as Director of Guest Services, a fancy title for him to keep the elderly upbeat and dancing.

Mac reached over the bar top and hugged Jenny.

"Thank you for renting out Mac's to celebrate your engagement." Mac turned to me and Oscar.

It wasn't like we hadn't celebrated the first time he had asked me, but we felt it was the right thing to do since he had asked my dad.

"We are happy that everyone came." Oscar looked out on the dance floor and broke out laughing.

It was fun to see Izzy trying to learn how to two-step, Gerald and Petunia trying to slow dance to a fast song with Orin between them, and Chandra swaying back and forth trying to keep her turban on. Even Mr. Prince Charming looked happy as he wagged his tail from one of the barstools near the dance floor.

Arabella could walk into any bar and fit in, but not the rest of us. And Amethyst was near the door, sitting on the new bouncer's lap that Max had hired, Ronnie, making sure no one crashed our private party. They had been inseparable since I had introduced them at this very spot.

"I'm so happy our two families have come to see eye-to-eye." Eloise sidled up next to us with Aunt Helena by her side.

"Not really eye-to-eye," Aunt Helena protested.

"Not now," I held my hand up and warned them not to start another fight here.

"I was going to say that we have come to terms that you and Oscar are going to have the wedding that you want and not what we want." Aunt Helena smiled and opened her arms wide.

"Thank you," I said and curled my arms around her, giving her a big squeeze. Even Oscar couldn't help himself. He got off the stool and gave each of the aunts a hug.

"There she is." The Marys stood at the door of the barn. Their eyes fell on me and they floated over. It seemed as though the mortals around us didn't even notice them.

"I understand the business contract for Gentle June's folded." Mary Ellen drummed her fingers together. The other Marys hovered over her. "According to the contract, if the company was sold while you were under contract, the new company was to purchase your lotion from you."

"What?" I jerked out of Aunt Helena's arms. Worry and fear punched me in the gut. There was no way I was going to give up Darla's recipe or the secret ingredient.

"But. . ." Mary Ellen stuck her finger out and wagged it in front of me. "Mac McGurtle worked his magic telling them that your product line never hit the stores and the bottles that did go out on the truck that morning were packaged in cheap plastic bottles which were not in the contract, therefore making the contract void."

A smile curved on my lips. My intuition told me Burt knew he was going to make Tiffany go down and he had deliberately used the plastic bottles so I could break the contract.

"You are one lucky spiritualist," Mary Lynn said before the Order of Elders disappeared into thin air.

"See," Oscar wrapped his arms around me again. "It's all working out."

We stood there for a minute looking at all of our friends gathered in one spot outside the borders of Whispering Falls celebrating the life between worlds that Oscar and I lived in.

"I love you, June Heal. And I can't wait for you to become my wife." Oscar's lips touched mine like a whisper.

Everything I had ever wanted was coming true. Even though my parents weren't physically there, I knew they were there in spirit and would be by my side during my wedding on All Hallows Eve.

Keep reading for a sneak peek of the next book in the series. A Charming Ghost is now available to purchase on Amazon or read for FREE in Kindle Unlimited.

BUT WAIT! Readers ask me how much my cozy mysteries and the characters in them reflect my real life. Well...here is a good story for you.

Whooo hooo!! I'm so glad we are a week out from last Coffee Chat with Tonya and happy to report the poison ivy is almost gone! But y'all we got more issues than Time magazine up in our family.

When y'all ask me if my real life ever creeps into books, well...grab your coffee because here is a prime example!

My sweet mom's birthday was over the weekend. Now, I'd already decided me and Rowena was going to stay there for a couple of extra days.

On her birthday, Sunday, Tracy and David were there too, and we were talking about what else...poison ivy! I was telling them how I can't stand not shaving my legs. Mom and Tracy told me they don't shave daily and I might've curled my nose a smidgen. And apparently it didn't go unnoticed.

I went inside the house to start cooking breakfast for everyone and mom went up to her room to get her bathing suit on and Tracy was with me. All the men were already outside on the porch.

The awfulest crash came from upstairs and my sister tore out of that kitchen like a bat out of hell and I kept flipping the bacon. My mom had fallen...shaving her legs!

Great. Now it's my fault.

Her wrist was a little stiff but she kept saying she was fine. We had a great day. We celebrated her birthday, swam, and had cake. When it came time for everyone to leave but me and Ro, I told mom that she should probably go get an x-ray because her wrist was a little swollen.

After a lot of coaxing, she agreed and I put my shoes on and told Tracy, David, and Eddy to go on home and we'd call them.

My mama looked me square in the face and said, "You're going with that top knot on your head?"

I said, "yes."

She sat back down in the chair and said, "I'm not going with you lookin' like that."

"Are you serious?" I asked.

"Yes. I'm dead serious. I'm not going with you looking like that. What if we see someone?" She was serious, y'all!

She protested against my hair!

Now...this is exactly like the southern mama's I write about! I looked at Eddy and he was laughing. Tracy and David were laughing and I said, "I can't wait until I tell my coffee chat people about this."

As you can see in the above photo, the before and after photo.

Yep...we went and she broke her wrist! Can you believe that? We were a tad bit shocked, and I'll probably be staying a few extra days (which will give us even more to talk about over coffee next week).

Oh...we didn't see anyone we knew so I could've worn my top knot! As I'm writing this, you can bet your bottom dollar my hair is pulled up in my top knot!

Okay, so y'all might be asking why I'm putting this little story in the back of my book, well, that's a darn tootin' good question.

This is exactly what you can expect when you sign up for my newsletter. There's always something going on in my life that I have to chat with y'all about each Tuesday on Coffee Chat with Tonya. Go to Tonyakappes.com and click on subscribe in the upper right corner to join.

SNEAK PEEK A CHARMING GHOST
BOOK 8

C hapter One

I WASN'T JUST COLD. I was bone-numbing, toe-curling, potion-freezing cold. And no amount of snuggling with Oscar, and I tried, was going to drive out the chill that had crept up into my soul. Deep into my soul.

I reached over and grazed Madame Torres, my crystal ball, with the pad of my finger. Her globe flashed red lightning bolts until it settled into a display that showed it was four-thirty in the morning. She wasn't about to show her face. My snarky crystal ball was not a morning person—I was sure it took hours for her to get all dolled up in her head turban and gobs of makeup she wore—and lightning bolts were her subtle way of telling me that she was not happy with the early morning wake-up call.

I glanced over at Oscar, my husband of two months. Only my white fairy-god cat was sitting between us with his eyes focused on me and his butt facing Oscar, which I was sure was on purpose.

My familiars, Mr. Prince Charming and Madame Torres, were still harboring hard feelings over my marriage to my best friend, Oscar Park. They were a little possessive of me.

"You too?" I asked and let out a heavy sigh.

He put a paw on my arm and I gave him a little scratch between his ears. White fur flew everywhere. He jerked away, turning toward Oscar. He jumped on Oscar's chest using it as a springboard off the bed and darted out the bedroom door.

"Ouch," Oscar groaned in a groggy voice and rubbed his chest before he turned on his right side and began to snore lightly.

The moonbeams dotted the walls of the bedroom through the window blinds giving me just enough light to see my handsome new husband. His black hair blended into the dark room but seeing his silhouette outlined by the moon made my insides bubble with happiness. Even after two months of marriage, I still wasn't used to the fact that I was finally Mrs. Oscar Park, though I kept my legal name of June Heal for business purposes.

I sighed when seeing Oscar slumber didn't ward off the soul freeze. I shivered. I glanced over to the closed blinds and wondered what kind of weather we were having. There was snow predicted and maybe that was the cold that had settled deep in my bones.

I loved how our village of Whispering Falls, Kentucky looked when it was blanketed in snow. I loved how it added a little coziness to my little homeopathic cure shop, A Charming Cure. I liked to think I helped people feel better in a natural kind of way. . .umm. . .maybe with a little help from my spiritual gift.

I'm blessed beyond belief with the spiritual gift of intuition, which helps me create the perfect cure for the customers who walk into my shop looking for the right homeopathic cure for them.

Some people might see me as a witch—a good one, mind you—but I liked to refer to myself as a spiritualist. It just sounds better. I was from the Good-Sider community of the witch world, meaning we only did magic for the good.

Meow, meow. Mr. Prince Charming stood at the bedroom door.

"I'm coming." I peeled back the covers and tiptoed out of the room.

There was a lot to do at the shop and a lot of generic potions to be made; lying in bed wide awake wasn't going to help get the shop ready for the town's second annual Winter Bazaar that was taking place in a couple of days.

Oscar didn't have to go into work until later in the day and he deserved to sleep in. He had been pulling double-duty as the sheriff of Whispering Falls and a deputy of Locust Grove, the town over, which was not a magical town like Whispering Falls.

Mr. Prince Charming's long tail happily danced in the air in front of me as I hurried down the hall to the combination kitchen and family room of my little cottage on the hill overlooking the village. I ran my hand along my orange couch on my way to push the button to my coffee maker. A good cup of hot magical beans was what I needed to get the chill out of my soul.

I looked out the window and smiled at the small flakes of snow. The wind rushed around with snow in its breath, blanketing the rooftops of all the small shops. The smell of freshly brewed coffee danced around my nose. I sucked in a deep breath, my eyes focused down the hill along Main Street where the gaslight carriage lights flickered between the holes in the pine needle wreaths that were hung for decoration.

Puffs of smoke curled into the air and danced in grey swirls in the moonlight.

I followed the swirls to the ground and watched as a lantern swung back and forth from Eloise Sandlewood's grasp.

She swung the chain to the right and keeping in the same time, she swung it to the left giving each shop a morning cleanse just as she did every morning by using her spiritual gift as an Incense Spiritualist.

Her long green velvet cloak dragged behind her with each deliberate step. The edges of her bright red hair peeked out from the hood, shielding her from the brisk wind and blowing snow.

Eloise was Oscar's aunt and now mine, though I had loved her long before she became family. She happened to have been my mother Darla's best friend during the small amount of time my mother had lived here. Darla was not a spiritualist and when my father had gotten killed in the line of duty, Darla and I moved to Locust Grove where she tried to raise me as a mortal. Oscar also grew up in Locust Grove across the street from us. I was in love with him since day one. Little did we realize we were destined to fall in love. Only he was a Dark-Sider Spiritualist which made it a little tricky for us to get married, but that was a whole other story.

It was all well and good until Darla had died and the spiritualists had come looking for me (and Oscar). Neither of us had any idea about our pasts nor of our powers.

I watched Eloise cleanse the village with loving memories of how she was able to help me understand where I had come from and share more about my mother.

Rowl. Mr. Prince Charming stood on his hind legs and planted his paws on the window. I leaned over a little more, getting a look at what he was staring at.

Eloise had stopped in front of Magical Moments, the flower shop, a little too long. Longer than usual. She was facing my little cottage on the hill.

Her emerald green eyes glowed, a red aura circled around them. It was as if she weren't present. Her red lips moved at warp speed and the smoke from the incense burner puffed like a freight train. She gripped the chain in her hand, swinging the chain higher and higher, clinking louder and louder, echoing throughout the mountainous town.

The coffee maker buzzed, making me jump and turn away from the trance Eloise had put me in. I sucked in a deep breath and straightened my shoulders. Mr. Prince Charming jumped off the counter. And I watched him as he circled my ankles doing his signature figure-eight move.

My eyes slid back up to the window and down the hill, but Eloise was gone. The backdrop of the mountains was filled with the purple dawn just beyond the horizon, leaving me with the sudden chill deep in my soul that had woken me from slumber.

Want to continue your magical journey? A CHARMING GHOST, book 8, is now available for purchase or in Kindle Unlimited.

If you enjoyed reading this book as much as I enjoyed writing it then be sure to return to the Amazon page and leave a review.

Go to Tonyakappes.com for a full reading order of my novels and while there join my newsletter. You can also find links to Facebook, Instagram and Goodreads.

Join like-minded readers like YOU in the Cozy Krew Facebook Group for dream casting, fan theories, and live Q & A's. It's like a BIG GIANT BOOK CLUB! But if you want to have your own book club, be sure you let me know! I love to send goodies.

Also By Tonya Kappes

A Camper and Criminals Cozy Mystery
BEACHES, BUNGALOWS, & BURGLARIES
DESERTS, DRIVERS, & DERELICTS
FORESTS, FISHING, & FORGERY
CHRISTMAS, CRIMINALS, & CAMPERS
MOTORHOMES, MAPS, & MURDER
CANYONS, CARAVANS, & CADAVERS
HITCHES, HIDEOUTS, & HOMICIDE
ASSAILANTS, ASPHALT, & ALIBIS
VALLEYS, VEHICLES & VICTIMS
SUNSETS, SABBATICAL, & SCANDAL
TENTS, TRAILS, & TURMOIL
KICKBACKS, KAYAKS, & KIDNAPPING
GEAR, GRILLS, & GUNS
EGGNOG, EXTORTION, & EVERGREENS
ROPES, RIDDLES, & ROBBERIES
PADDLERS, PROMISES, & POISON
INSECTS, IVY, & INVESTIGATIONS
OUTDOORS, OARS, & OATHS
WILDLIFE, WARRANTS, & WEAPONS
BLOSSOMS, BARBEQUE, & BLACKMAIL
LANTERNS, LAKES, & LARCENY
JACKETS, JACK-O-LANTERN, & JUSTICE
SANTA, SUNRISES, & SUSPICIONS
VISTAS, VICES, & VALENTINES
ADVENTURE, ABDUCTION, & ARREST
RANGERS, RV'S, & REVENGE
CAMPFIRES, COURAGE, & CONVICTS
TRAPPING, TURKEYS, & THANKSGIVING
GIFTS, GLAMPING, & GLOCKS
ZONING, ZEALOTS, & ZIPLINES

HAMMOCKS, HANDGUNS, & HEARSAY

Kenni Lowry Mystery Series
FIXIN' TO DIE
SOUTHERN FRIED
AX TO GRIND
SIX FEET UNDER
DEAD AS A DOORNAIL
TANGLED UP IN TINSEL
DIGGIN' UP DIRT
BLOWIN' UP A MURDER

Killer Coffee Mystery Series
SCENE OF THE GRIND
MOCHA AND MURDER
FRESHLY GROUND MURDER
COLD BLOODED BREW
DECAFFEINATED SCANDAL
A KILLER LATTE
HOLIDAY ROAST MORTEM
DEAD TO THE LAST DROP
A CHARMING BLEND NOVELLA (CROSSOVER WITH MAGICAL
CURES MYSTERY)
FROTHY FOUL PLAY
SPOONFUL OF MURDER
BARISTA BUMP-OFF
CAPPUCCINO CRIMINAL

Holiday Cozy Mystery
FOUR LEAF FELONY
MOTHER'S DAY MURDER
A HALLOWEEN HOMICIDE
NEW YEAR NUISANCE
CHOCOLATE BUNNY BETRAYAL

APRIL FOOL'S ALIBI
FATHER'S DAY MURDER
THANKSGIVING TREACHERY
SANTA CLAUSE SURPRISE

Mail Carrier Cozy Mystery
STAMPED OUT
ADDRESS FOR MURDER
ALL SHE WROTE
RETURN TO SENDER
FIRST CLASS KILLER
POST MORTEM
DEADLY DELIVERY
RED LETTER SLAY

Magical Cures Mystery Series
A CHARMING CRIME
A CHARMING CURE
A CHARMING POTION (novella)
A CHARMING WISH
A CHARMING SPELL
A CHARMING MAGIC
A CHARMING SECRET
A CHARMING CHRISTMAS (novella)
A CHARMING FATALITY
A CHARMING DEATH (novella)
A CHARMING GHOST
A CHARMING HEX
A CHARMING VOODOO
A CHARMING CORPSE
A CHARMING MISFORTUNE
A CHARMING BLEND (CROSSOVER WITH A KILLER COFFEE COZY)
A CHARMING DECEPTION

A Southern Magical Bakery Cozy Mystery Serial
A SOUTHERN MAGICAL BAKERY

A Ghostly Southern Mystery Series
A GHOSTLY UNDERTAKING
A GHOSTLY GRAVE
A GHOSTLY DEMISE
A GHOSTLY MURDER
A GHOSTLY REUNION
A GHOSTLY MORTALITY
A GHOSTLY SECRET
A GHOSTLY SUSPECT

A Southern Cake Baker Series
(WRITTEN UNDER MAYEE BELL)
CAKE AND PUNISHMENT
BATTER OFF DEAD

Spies and Spells Mystery Series
SPIES AND SPELLS
BETTING OFF DEAD
GET WITCH or DIE TRYING

A Laurel London Mystery Series
CHECKERED CRIME
CHECKERED PAST
CHECKERED THIEF

A Divorced Diva Beading Mystery Series
A BEAD OF DOUBT SHORT STORY
STRUNG OUT TO DIE
CRIMPED TO DEATH

Olivia Davis Paranormal Mystery Series

SPLITSVILLE.COM
COLOR ME LOVE (novella)
COLOR ME A CRIME

Grandberry Falls Books
THE LADYBUG JINX
HAPPY NEW LIFE
A SUPERSTITIOUS CHRISTMAS
NEVER TELL YOUR DREAMS

About Tonya

Tonya has written over 100 novels, all of which have graced numerous bestseller lists, including the USA Today. *Best known for stories charged with emotion and humor and filled with flawed characters, her novels have garnered reader praise and glowing critical reviews. She lives with her husband and a very spoiled rescue cat named Ro. Tonya grew up in the small southern Kentucky town of Nicholasville. Now that her four boys are grown men, Tonya writes full-time in her camper she calls her SHAMPER (she-camper).*

Learn more about her be sure to check out her website tonyakappes.com. Find her on Facebook, Twitter, BookBub, and Instagram

Sign up to receive her newsletter, where you'll get free books, exclusive bonus content, and news of her releases and sales.

If you liked this book, please take a few minutes to leave a review now! Authors (Tonya included) really appreciate this, and it helps draw more readers to books they might like. Thanks!

Cover artist: Mariah Sinclair: The Cover Vault

Made in the USA
Las Vegas, NV
08 May 2023

71742261R00095

Bubble... Bubble... Whispering Falls' resident potion maker, June Heal, is the first witch in the magical village to make a big money deal with the Head To Toe Works, a national chain specializing in spa and natural products.

CURES AND TROUBLE... June is going to need to use her own stress relief potion she made especially for Head To Toe Works after she discovers the dead body of Burt Rossen, the co-owner of Head To Toe Works, on the belt of the assembly line of her stress free lotion product.

MAGIC STIRS... A new baby is born in Whispering Falls and giving Oscar Park, June's fiancé and Whispering Falls' sheriff, the itch to get a wedding date set and gives June an ultimatum.

AND TROUBLES DOUBLE... June is forced to use her witchy ways to figure out who stole her secret potion after it turns up missing. Rumors are flying around like broomsticks that June is a witch and used a spell to murder Mr. Rossen. Someone wants her out of Head To Toe Works, but who? Will the killer get to June before she can walk down the aisle?

www.tonyakappes.com

ISBN 9781514648452